Weird Works

Of

Dave Martel

The Bizarchives

Copyright © 2023 by Dave Martel

All rights reserved.

No part of this book may be reproduced in any form or by any electronic or mechanical means, including information storage and retrieval systems, without written permission from the author, except for the use of brief quotations in a book review.

Contents

Foreword	vii
Into the Dreamsea	1
Lands Beyond Dreams	3
Song of the Merfolk	5
From Space it Came Falling	7
Phantom of Black Lake	9
Artist's Trance	11
Krampusnacht	13
Malthereal Swarm	14
Coming Age of the Purple Moon	16
Replicant Form	18
The Boglord's Curse	20
The Yawning Chasm	23
Nümanity Burns	25
Twas the Night Before Christmas	28
Warrior's Dance	32
Gnomish Knell *From Toadstool Magazine Issue #1*	33
Glorious Spring *From Toadstool Magazine Issue #3*	35
Momma's Love	37
On Depression *Short Essay*	39
My Decay	41
Riversong	43
Winter Solemn	44
Mother Pennsylvania	45
When the Darkness Came to Town	48
Parables of the Biomancer *From Aegeon Sci-fi Illustrated Issue #2*	51
Welcome *Introduction to The Bizarchives Issue #1*	61

The Silver Key *Introduction to The Bizarchives Issue #2*	64
Lex and the Odd Village *From The Bizarchives Issue #2*	70
Lex and the Horror of Bernwick Hollows *From The Bizarchives Issue #2*	82
Lex and the Lost Girl *From The Bizarchives Issue #1*	94
Lex Conquers Hell *From The Bizarchives Issue #3*	101
She Has Arrived *From The Bizarchives Issue #4*	115
They Never Woke Up *From The Bizarchives Issue $1*	130
Human Candles	137
Thank you for reading	161

The Bizarchives
Weird Tales of Monsters, Magic, and Machines

Presented by
The Midgard Institute
of Science Fiction & Fantasy Literature

Foreword
By Tristan Powers

The Weird Works of Dave Martel is a fascinating and creative plunge into the depths of a hitherto largely abandoned and nearly forgotten genre of literary material which was, at one time, perhaps the most popular example of mass market production made during the modern era. Hearkening back to the roots of Pulp and Weird Fiction and its origins in distinguished and acclaimed artists such as H. P. Lovecraft and his Cthulhu Mythos, Robert E. Howard and his Conan series which is widely reputed to have originated the entire genre of Sword and Sorcery itself, or Edgar Rice Burroughs and his innovative and fascinating glimpses of the future of technology and its impacts upon man and the soul, combined with his patented flair for the classical adventure.

The ghoulish, fantastical and kaleidoscopic stories featured in Weird Works are a loving homage to a genre of the past written in the talented hand of a modern artist who has taken great pains and time to look back and analyze these great classical authors and reproduce stories in their mold, that they would themselves have enjoyed and which could have been published alongside their own magazines and eagerly gobbled up by the likes of our great grandparents.These works are produced in true vein of the classic example and with no alterations and filters applied to make them more in vogue with modern society and its changing pop-culture scene. These are not the Netflix adaptations of the golden works retold for a new generation, but the true blood itself, distilled and refined for the purpose of allowing the new generation to appreciate one of the defining and most spectacular periods of literature to ever be devised.

Weird Works can be broken into a few different categories of material, each emblematic of a particular subgenre of pulp or style of associated literature. From the visceral sonorous tones of "into the dreamsea" we are catapulted into the sort of heady but unpretentious and hearthrumming poetry that characterizes the rest of the material, and serves as the greatest of thematic openings for its impressive collection. "Song of the Merfolk" and "From Space it Came Falling" exemplify the range of thematic diversity contained in this collection, shifting from Lovecraftian-esque uncanny terrors of man, to the horror-scifi imagery of the hostile depths of space and interplanetary invasions. "The Boglord's Curse" represents a definitive foray into the poetry of quasi-mystical adventure and esoteric horror that would not be considered out of place in the greatest works of the genre, to be read in concert with Clark Ashton Smith, Arthur Conan Doyle or Jules Verne.

The short essay "on depression" might strike some as intimate and uncomfortable, but one of the defining elements of artistic thought is the emotional insight to reach deep within the self and pull out night terrors, hags and anxieties and use them to paint a canvas of meaning and beauty with them. In this Mr. Martel has succeeded I think, and I would urge readers

FOREWORD

to not skip this section no matter how uncomfortable - and perhaps relatable - you may find it.

"Parables of the Biomancer" begins the section of short stories and longer narrative prose work, of which Weird Works has collected some of the best modern examples in the space. Ranging from bio-horror to classical sword and sorcery, these stories are sure to thrill and chill at equal measure any reader who is lucky enough to give them a thorough reading. The "Lex" series, of which the author should rightfully account his magnum opus and shining diamond among glittering gems, contains the first four of these branching narrative treasures all set with the same main character and in the same world. Lex clearly takes conscious inspiration from the patriarch of sword and sorcery fiction himself, Robert E. Howard and his Conan series, though with notable uniqueness and characterization. The World of Lex is a terrifying and action packed place showing influences in historical realities of medieval and dark age europe, existing and ancient folk tales and stories, and the living germanic faith of its author, to produce a stunning and breathtaking example of the genre. It can be said with no lack of consideration that these works are my personal favorite and I would urge them upon any of today's early readers, for truly the character of Lex will take his place with Conan and Kane and Kull, Faffhrd, the Mouser, and Elric in the annals of history and public prestige, and this early collection will be highly sought after in the distant future in light of it.

Weird Works can be considered most strikingly as a homage to the infamous "Weird Tales" magazine running in its heyday from 1922-1938 and which published the material of the Cthulhu Mythos, Conan, and the works of Clark Ashton Smith. Although never gauchely derivative, Weird Works is inestimably indentured to this golden age of Pulp and Weird Fiction, and any enjoyers of this esteemed media or those inestimable men and women of the modern age who possess the blood of heroes, a mind of madness or a morbid soul from the realms beyond shall find a welcome home in Weird Works.

May we come to read ever yet more volumes of adventure, insight and resolute terror.

Into the Dreamsea

I've dreamt black thirst of vengeance
Carried by hateful wings
To ebon moons of far-flung worlds
Where goatish devils sing

I've plunged jagged chasm voids
That vomit molten earth
Geysers belching bile bursts
Steaming vile birth

I've thrusted sharpened blades
Into a thousand breasts
Relish every time I see
The panicked eyes of death

I care not for the luxuries
Of song and silk and feast
Gift me stampeding choired hate
Of a hundred hungered beasts

Take me to the shaman's grove
With hung corpses on display
Frenzied dances, bloody rites
Forgotten magic ways

Then pass me ghastly goblets
Forged from wizards' bones
Let the elixir melt my mind
As I sit on broken thrones

Teach me long lost legends
Scryed on long lost tombs
In the blood of slaughtered kings
Who met untimely dooms

Then I return to mundane world
With maddened magic tales
And write them down for others
For the dreamsea they may sail

Lands Beyond Dreams

Beneath shifting worlds
Lies a place of strange wonder
Where calamity unfurls
Tears twilight asunder

Subnormal and twisted
Beyond comprehension
Black heavens betwixt it
No tongue dares its mention

Liquid nightmares flow forth
Aqueducts forged from flesh
Through forests of black swords
Living trees scream and stretch

Maddened men wander
Minds wracked with disease
Dark mysteries pondered
But never conceived

Cerulean skies overhead
Soar beasts of red feather
With cyclopean heads
And claws that can sever

Great bellowing howls
Of Mastodonic primates
Pink slime on their jowls
From the men that they ate

Endlessly spanned
Where chaos' teem
In the lands beyond lands
In the dreams beyond dreams

Song of the Merfolk

Lurk in the depths
Of seas below
Our race has kept
What no one knows

Human face
Flesh of scale
Below the waist
Fish-like tail

Milky eyes
Fang'ed maw
On arms at side
Webb'ed claw

Fertilizing slimy sacks
Hatchlings spewing forth
Articulating spiny backs
Writhing tongue splits a'fork

If lost at sea, you soon will be
Darkest depths dragged down
From land to lea, tell tales of me
Of sailors slowly drowned

Half of you become our meat
Others are our tithe
To cosmic beings who soundly sleep
'Til their æon they arise

They came to earth long before
From realms of void so vast
Raised us from our lowly form
To breed a servant caste

Man thinks himself earthly kings
But his power slowly wanes
our slumbering sires soon will bring
An age where earth will change

Soon your cities will crumble down
Beneath the mammoth waves
And the Merfolk race will don the crown
With mankind as our slaves

From Space it Came Falling

Here trees grow sideward
A forest unnatural
Lifeforce perverted
Spirits be wrathful

Warping wood wilds
Disorder of time
See nature defiled
No reason or rhyme

Foul feral forms
Creatures grow twisted
White fangs and black horns
Know not what bewitched them

Brackish bogs birthing
Baleful black beasts
Slithered slime surfing
Foul floating foam yeast

From space it came falling
Strange hues from it glowing
To all things it's calling
Strange forces come flowing

Critters now hateful
Hungered for flesh
They feast on each other
And from their own nests

Rapidly spreading
Land falling ill
Malforming the world
To its alien will

Purple skies moan
Air reeks of strange sour
It replicated its home
And Earth's been devoured

Phantom of Black Lake

The phantom takes flight
As darkness sets in
Wailing women in white
Moan ghoulish black hymns

Vaguely human in form
It shifts in its shape
Cool waters turn warm
On ancient black lake

Cultists entranced
On lakeshores of grey shale
Clasping cold hands
Cry chorused queer wails

Through eons and ages
Phantasm laid wait
Calling witches and mages
To open its gate

Twitching, distending
Bones cracking, deformed
Spasms, limbs bending
Blood mists from their pores

Crimson clouds fill the sky
Howls of unspeakable pain
Twisted bodies sucked dry
Their corpses all drained

The phantom has drank
Of those whom it leered
Back to black lake it sank
For a thousand more years

Artist's Trance

Hoist the pen
Garner the ink
Your mind ascend
And body sink

Colors dance
Stories tell
Artist's trance
Wordless spell

Heroes depicted
Unconquerable odds
Entities wicked
Face muscular Gods

Dimensions unhinge
Fragments of dreams
Where elvenfolk sing
And foul demons scream

Slathering paint
Fantasy born
Shapeless take shape
And formless take form

Drunk with creation
A frenzy poetic
Strange demonstration
Birthing aesthetic

Depleted, exhausted
Completed and formal
Vision metamorphosed
creation immortal

Krampusnacht

From ironwood, of thurses-born
Of cloven hoof and gnarled horn
From ancient times long forgot
Called again by hearts of rot
Into our world this devil came
Now we learn this devil's name
Krampus! Krampus! Please leave us be!
We did not know! We could not see!
We only lived as we were taught!
The vice and greed that we all sought
The Krampus comes as daylight fades
A price for nið that children paid
If Yuletide comes with hearts of black
A song to harken Krampus back
To truly find who Krampus is
In your mirror's glass the reflection's his

Malthereal Swarm

I gaze deeply into the blackest black
And witness forms arcane
Phantom nails my brain awrack
Ancient tongues curse profane

Amoebic shadows writhe and rot
Twist and fold upon themselves
From a realm that man forgot
Beneath abyssal purple hells

I lean before the scrying glass
A waking eldritch dream
Horrid songs and spells acast
To beckon things obscene

The mirror's misty mystery
My melting mind malformed
The barren black so blissfully
Renders me reborn

What was me, no longer is
In my soul the larvae bore
A willing host so onerous
Sailing from this mortal shore

My psychic depth, a fertile womb
From bursting skull they hatch
Amorphous nameless crawling doom
All parts of me detach

Nirvanic state where life dissolves
Reality unweaves
Humanity, a problem solved
Go forth my brood, it's time to feed

Coming Age of the Purple Moon

The sun sinks behind the crest
Never to rise again
Blackness draped from east to west
Last lights begin to wane

Men are wracked with panicked fright
Earth now a shadowed tomb
Begins the age of endless night
And the ascending purple moon

Pallid glare of purple stare
Gleams in the moaning dark
Wailing whispers haunt the air
Sanity torn apart

Phantom forms swim sunless skies
Sing songs with cadence foul
Maddened men's helpless cries
Enchanted by the howls

Can no longer trust what is seen
What was there now is not
Blurring senses, waking dream
As psyche starts to rot

Enemies false perceived
Memories wrong recalled
Ghostly whispers, minds deceived
Paranoia poisons all

A purple hell, the oceans swell
Rivers are reversed
Time is torn and tales will tell
Of earth in cosmic curse

From oldest depths of ground and sea
Ghastly structures stab the skies
Geometry of blasphemy
Cause bleeding human eyes

Titanic ebon gates cast wide
They take many-wing'd flight
Over this realm they now preside
Their kingdom of purple night

Replicant Form

This form unborn and replicant
With locking eyeless gaze
Appendages emerging bent
In uncanniest of ways

In caution I retreat my steps
It mirrors them in kind
While learning it appears inept
becomes flawless human mime

Its visage shines with nameless hues
It spasms then retracts
Sprouting flesh and innards fuse
Into a human form intact

Jaws unhinge from rigid face
Casts subaural droning screech
Evolving into its pupal phase
Its first attempts at speech

Replicant Form

It crawled out of unworldly womb
From a realm we cannot see
Now it stands in this empty room
A more perfect form of me

The Boglord's Curse

Clinging viridescent fog
Haunted marsh moist with mold
Slime and sludge and stagnant sog
Which lies beyond the rolling wold

Into the bog, deep and dank
Sits nature's cruelest ward
His form forlorn and grim and lank
A dreary dreadful lord

His mind a morbid force to see
Sealing secrets unrecant
Sinful songs and sorceries
Among the mists a murling chant

Swirling seer, a psychopomp
One that weaves your fate
Unfurling here, in frightful swamp
Kniving words he doth spake

Art they true? Or art they false?
Strange visions wrack my brain
From unseen subpsychic vaults
Putrid futures he proclaims

Dreams bleed as time decays
Morning moons and sun at dusk
Nights dissolve to darkened days
My spirit flees my fleshy husk

I sink into the murky mud
A fetal fluid sack
Embryonic ooze and blood
Chthonic morphing black

Hairless, wretched milky form
Emerge from pulsing slime
Into a realm with stars adorned
Cosmic colors so sublime

Soaring psychedelic flares
Billions of us float
Infantile helpless bairns
Suspended womb-like boats

Towards the source of yawning light
Drifting gently against our will
Devouring void of blinding bright
Millions swallowed, never filled

Roots as spines and vines as veins
Bark as skin in fetal form
Thoughtless minds, forgotten names
Betwixt our world, dimensions torn

My time has come, my turn is nigh
The great source shall drink me whole
No fear is felt, no urge to cry
I surrender to it my sourdine soul

Thrust into a twisting storm
Of countless fragment thoughts
Burning cold and frigid warm
Astral nets nightmares caught

Past and present and future melt
Things known but lost to time
Dooms weaved but never dealt
In shattered schizo rhyme

Crescendo in a blaring blur
Left a shaking broken shell
Lying nude in the swampy slur
Without a tale to tell

I sit and rock, repeating verse
From vision with no memory
It seems that the Boglord's ancient curse
Is revealing what we cannot see

The Yawning Chasm

The chasm it yawns
A void of dark depths
Since the primordial dawns
Its secrets have kept

It groans and it grinds
An endless dull roar
It moans and it whines
From unknowable core

Men venture beneath
But never return
Their wives left to weep
They never do learn

Never escape
This hideous black maw
Forever agape
Earth's ancient black jaws

Tales have been told
Of what lies thereunder
Hoards of lost gold
And devils that slumber

A realm so chthonic
Men could not fathom
Under spires of onyx
Within yawning chasm

Nümanity Burns

Cough, hack
Lungs collapse
Insides turn black
Leaking pink sap

Contagion infecting
Carcasses stink
Concoctions injecting
Chaos' brink

Propaganda machine
Cult-like devotion
Truth now obscene
Panicked emotion

Drink of our pain
Reduce us to filth
Life they disdain
Fattened and milked

Needles and probes
Mutation looming
Rewriting the code
Which defines human

Hairless and sexless
Genetics assembled
Societal sepsis
Change incremental

Heretics scorned
Cut from the vine
The natural born
Expelled for our crimes

Parallel lives
Foundations rebuilt
Outside of the hives
Agrarian ilk

Ancestral mode
Proles we return
Penance is owed
System must burn

Through the dark
The naturals survive
Remember the art
Traditions revive

Machine starts to rot
Deep at its core
In safety forgot
How to wage war

We bring iron beasts
Steel dragons on high
Ashen black sleet
Falls from the sky

Subhumans protect
Beloved complex
Destiny set
Devoid of regret

True born men
Clad in new steel
Through streets descend
Bring them to heel

Lined against walls
Facing their fate
Last curtain call
Skulls blown agape

Nature's true will
Grim beauty behold
On rubble rebuild
A new age of gold

Twas the Night Before Christmas

Twas the night before Christmas
And all through the home
Silent songs of still slumber
As the family laid prone

But from a dark place
The mad void between stars
Descended a cruel form
Beyond Carcosa and Mars

Eons before now
It sailed with strange thrust
It burrowed its girth
In Earth's ancient red crust

It slept there in wait
For ages untold
Through tectonic shifts
And long glacial cold

But now on this night
By the glow of yule moon
It pulsates and blooms
From alien cocoon

In haunting night fog
It emerges bereft
It spits and it gurgles
With its first yawning breath

The quaint Christmas home
Beckons the beast
The scent of soft flesh
A call to its feast

Striking down from the skies
With terrible clatter
A shimmering spear
Made sprays of red splatter

In pain it recoils
As blood starts to flow
Its eyespots blinded
By radiant glow

From the gold aura
Steps a man strong and fair
With crimson white robes
And silvering hair

With a ho, ho, ho
His belly doth shake
He raised his gloved fist
Santa doth spake

"How dare you emerge
With your form so profane
On this holiest of nights
My sacred domain"

"In that humble house
Sleeps men of pure heart
If you take one more step
I shall tear you apart!"

The creature gave snarl
And lunged him right forth
But Santa dodged swiftly
And countered with force

"Begone foul devil!
Go back to your tomb
On this night I gift presents
But to you I give doom!"

The battle ensued
Flashed magic and steel
Victorious was Santa
Brought the monster to heel

But morning then came
snowfall like white silk
All the cookies were eaten
And drank was the milk

The children lept up
Howling with glee
When they saw the bounty
Under the tree

So Christmas was merry
And filled with true joy
Nestled by hearthfire
With blankets and toys

But never they knew
About what came from beneath
Or that Santa Claus, the jolly Christmas elf
Was a slayer of beasts

Warrior's Dance

A dance of dark blades
Shall dash you to death
Gasp as life fades
Splits open your breast

Swirling and whirling
Bright flashes of steel
Deaths door unfurling
Brings heroes to heel

Silver light blinding
Puts cowards in trance
Soon a grave finding
When warriors dance

Gnomish Knell
From Toadstool Magazine Issue #1

Suckle the prickle buckle vine
Sip the drips of the wild wine
Down the gullet to belly brine
To soften the soul with mild mind

Dance and sway as songs beplay
Longest days of wrongest ways
Soon begone to dawn betray
a night so gay in moonlight stay

Wine and women and pleasured glee
In harrowed hallows of treasured trees
Sorrowed sights no longer seen
Disrobe your troubles and follow me

Into the purple magic mists
Where holy earth and mirth betwixt
Planes mundane swirling twist
Where dreams become a surest wish

Lose yourself in gnomish spell
Leave behind the hueless hell
Hear the flutes and tales we tell
In the ancient gnomish knell

Glorious Spring
From Toadstool Magazine Issue #3

Green is freed from frigid greed
By the smile of the sun
Bulbs and blossoms and sprouting seeds
As winter is on the run

Awake my dear, our sleep is done
The Snow and ice are gone
It's time for work and time for fun
Plant the fern and call the faun

Redcap house and redcap hats
Don your leaf-green slacks
Red-brown shoes freshly waxed
Foraged mushrooms in our sacks

Bumbles buzzing in fluttered flight
Honeycombs golden drip
Shining morns and dew-kissed nights
Wild wines and spirits sipped

Rafters hanging drying leaf
Stuff to stoke our pipes
Toking puffs bring nigh relief
A lovely lazy life

Blow the flute and bang the drum
In the sunshine sing
It's time for work and time for fun
And time for glorious spring

Momma's Love

Pulled from otherworld to the light
In her womb so warm
Hours of pain through she fights
Body worn and torn

Exhausted breaths, tears of love
First time she sees our face
Swears an oath to Gods above
Love's truest warm embrace

Pitter patter, little feet
We grow as time blows by
She ensures our clothes are neat
Comforts when we cry

She blinks once, we start to talk
Again we sleep alone
She blinks thrice, we start to walk
Soon we leave her home

Momma looks on at her boys
As they grow to men
She cherishes our old toys
And remembers way back when

She sits so proud as we wed
Loves grandkids as her own
Makes sure we all stay fed
And love is all we're shown

But father time has his way
Life is precious short
Soon mom begins to grey
And is called to heaven's court

Her whole life she gives her heart
And gives her damnedest try
That's why life's hardest part
Is when we have to say goodbye

On Depression
Short Essay

This following poem was written during the depths of a bad depression episode. The pandemic lockdowns took everything from me. My wife and I were preparing to buy our first house together. I had a job that I was at for 6 years and saved up a nest egg. Our third child, my daughter Helena was about to be born. Then lockdowns came.

I lost my job and my savings dwindled away to nothing. All of our dreams of owning a home, after years of living with relatives, in rundown apartments and garages, were crushed. I generally get seasonal depression where I start to go into "hibernation mode" in the middle of winter and lose motivation. But rarely does it come with dark thoughts.

Those two years were the worst of my life. I put on a ton of weight, my health went to hell and the anxiety of a looming plague while my wife was pregnant really corrupted my mind. The isolation on top of everything made it worse.

I almost didn't put this poem in here because it makes me sick to read it. I feel embarrassed and ashamed by it. Disgusted that I ever let myself get to that point. It's pathetic and revolting. It's almost as if someone else wrote it. Not me, but a twisted form of me possessed by wicked forces.

But alas, many folks that are of creative mind have dark episodes. And when you descend into those shadowy realms you can retrieve something beautiful. It's very Odinic. The Allfather was pinned to the world tree for nine days, sacrificing himself unto himself in order to learn the secret of the runes. He then shared it with all of us.

So, if you're reading this and you have one of these depressive states, and go into a dark place in your mind. Don't waste it. Treat it as an initiation of sorts. An esoteric journey. Create something meaningful while you're down there. And after you rise again, share it with others to bring them happiness and inspiration.

Use your sorrow to help cure others of theirs.

My Decay

All around decays entropic
My hands feel heavy as stone
No strength nor will enough to stop it
Even crowded rooms I feel alone

My body rots, my mind a blur
Toxic thoughts and hueless haze
Nights bleed oft into the days
I wish it was the way it were

I love my children more than life
I'm not a father but a curse
Endless disappointment for my wife
As my state gets slowly worse

My body bulges, I'm losing teeth
Nightmares vivid, never sleep
Recurring sickness, forever weak
I can't control the way I eat

My flame flickers, soon going out
Poets are worth more when dead
Maybe with this pistol in my mouth
It'll heal the nails within my head

I would've left long ago
But I fear my children's pain
So I fight this demon they call woe
And pull the anchor up by the chain

Riversong

The silent roar, its gentle might.
At mercy, both sand and stone.
Carving clay to wash away
It's bed, an earthen throne.

The veins of life, world renown
Bounteous are her gifts.
Treacherous can be, like storm and sea.
Many have gone amiss.

At rising dawn when all's serene.
I listen morning-long.
Her healing hum, since time begun.
The enchanting riversong.

Winter Solemn

The whispering dance of northern breeze
    beckons haunting chill.
At weeping stance the ash trees sway lost in
    nightly still.
Cold caress encircles, flesh and coils around my
    spine.
A lonely guest among nobles dressed, the frost
    upon the pines.

Mother Pennsylvania

From the mighty Susquehanna
To Allegheny flowing free
Born of ol' Appalachia
Mountains painted sea of green

My father's fathers were all born here
Steely boys, mountain bred
Couldn't read nor write ,their own names
But in every war they gladly bled

Little thanks did they get
For all the battles that they won
Stockboss said "get back to work!"
There ain't no time to mourn for sons

Momma drank whiskey every night
Until she died alone
She never healed from when stockboss said
Your boys ain't coming home

They got crushed down under earth
They screamed but couldn't be saved
But the company's gonna keep their checks
Because they ain't alive to get their pay

This went on for many years
Until we broke our yoke
Coalmine barons done pushed too far
Got repaid with rifle smoke

Mother Pennsylvania
Embraced us all with love
We lived and farmed as free ol' boys
Praise to Gods above

But now the piglets have grown to hogs
And getting rowdy in their roosts
The baron's kids are back again
Asking for the noose

Mother Pennsylvania

They called us backwards way back then
Now we're "racist" they all say
Bourgeois lies from faggot thieves
To take our land away

These yuppies think they can pull one on me
Well they can surely try
Like my father's fathers that came before
For Mother Pennsylvania,
I will gladly die.

When the Darkness Came to Town

I remember the time and day
When the darkness came to town
We weren't alone in this pain
It hit the folks from all around

It started out as funny pills
Then to shooting tar
Boys went from hometown kids
To breaking into cars

I remember watching all my kin
Lose the life behind their eyes
No twenty something with life to live
Deserves to rot alive

I can't stomach no more funerals
And I'm sorry for what it's worth
But I can't watch another mom cry
As her baby's dropped into the earth

My little brother spent his youth in prison
And half my buddies are all dead
My kids will never meet Uncle Drew
Joe will never see his daughter wed

Yuppies all just sneer and mock
Say we're privileged cause we're white
But ignored the sirens screaming by
Collecting bodies every night

My kinsman lost his father
Then his stepdad and little bro
I'm very proud he made it out
Even though progress is slow

We're older now and better now
My folks are mostly clean
But forever burned into my mind
Is who made money off that scheme

Big Pharma corpo royalty
Sackler, that's their name
Made billions off our suffering
Our lives were just a game

Behind their cozy mansion walls
Living easy, sipping wine
They think that they can't be touched
A rifle slug could reach just fine

I ain't saying about doing shit
Just throwing things around
But maybe someday a heartbroke dad
Could bring darkness to their town

Parables of the Biomancer
From Aegeon Sci-Fi Illustrated Issue #2

For centuries mankind wallowed in his own puddle of anxiety. Perplexed by the looming consequences of their own design. Before I enlightened them, these self-anointed apes couldn't seem to conjure the basic logic to claw their way from their terminal descent of cyclical failure. Scarcity of resources leading to suffering then a technological solution consuming evermore resources leading to more scarcity and more suffering. Their infatuation with polymer and steel, oil and lumber. All of which draining an already emaciated earth, to which they puked the vile byproducts back into her bosom, poisoning her. Despite the fetishes of transhumanist technophiles, the solution is and always has been beneath mankind's nose. There is a resource far more abundant, accessible and renewable than petroleum, plastics or hemp. It is a resource that has liberated us from archaic circuit boards and simplistic scripts and neural networks.

You see, technophiles fantasized about a singularity. A point where man merged with machine into some metamechanical apotheosis. Transcending his form and lowly quasiconscious state into godlike awareness and existence. Despite appearing in opposition to theists of old, both clung onto man's pathetic presupposition that there is a supranatural state of being for either Gods or man. I have humbled them both.

The tech fetishists' folly came in that their petty dreams were hamstrung by the resources and scarcity they aimed to escape. Foolish to believe they could liberate themselves from this techno-samsara using the very chains that imprisoned them. And as time went on the more fanatical they became as their endeavors brought only more societal retardation and decay. They dreamed of an enlightened utopia but only seemed to muster more trinkets to satisfy their carnal thirsts. The higher the tech, the more lowly and bestial they became. Within a cell constructed of their own ill begotten hubris they protested by rattling their shackles ever louder. But with every cry their manacles tightened and the more delusional they became. It was I who saved them from their own misery. It was I who offered them salvation.

There never was a possible merger with machines. This concept within itself is a paradox. An amusingly unsolvable conundrum. Man could never merge with machine for he was already a machine. There was no exterior resource required to fuel the biomechanical revolution for there was a resource that was more sculptable, renewable and versatile than any we have seen before. Not only was this material exceedingly abundant, we had it in excess. Flesh. Organic matter and its countless preassembled forms. Enamel of bones and teeth proved superior to concrete, lumber and plastics. Robotics were easily overtaken by general biomechanics, human limbs and their exquisite articulation can complete fine motor tasks far better than any hamfisted hydraulics. And finally, the fumbled attempts at quantum computing pale in comparison to the computational power of the human brain.

Technology has always been marching towards this final culmination. Not a merger of man and machine but the epiphany that man is machine. The final disregard of his antiquated moral obstacles. Morals they abandoned æons before but continued to regurgitate, a facade hiding their ego. In ages past I would have been bound and burned alive for commodifying the human body. While unenlightened, at least these primitive peoples had conviction. The liberals and humanists of the subsequent postindustrial ages abandoned this belief that man's form is of divine construction and placed their own condition upon the throne of God as their highest ideal. A most fortuitous ideological development as their insincerity was easily subverted. It didn't take long for them to accept that the human body holds no sacred qualities and we are obligated to harvest it at will. Flesh is a resource as any other. Their concern was simply free access to pleasure and status. A few bribes of comfort and by sunrise the technophiles were willing biomechanical revolutionaries.

In contrast, theists proved much more stubborn. Despite the abject degeneration of their held superstitions from olden times, they clung to these superstitions nonetheless. Although naive, this stout opposition in favor of their last shreds of belief was commendable to some extent. The last pure bastion of primeval man. The steadfast conquering spirit of the ancient world. And like their ancestors before they had to be broken and demoralized. To prove the supremacy of my innovations I genetically assembled all of their prophets. I paraded them through the streets and watched as the believers rejoiced. Hurling themselves at the feet of my creations like bewildered lambs. Christ, Buddha, Mohammed, Zoroaster and others. In the flesh, walking among them. Mindless golems of my construction. After the fanfare I brought them back to my laboratory, butchered them and reassembled them into a chimeric monstrosity. A beautifully grotesque testament to my mastery over nature and coup de grace of antiquity's final breath. They now float helplessly in a tube of revitalization serum keeping them alive just enough for them to feel the anguish of their existence. A constant reminder that I have enslaved their Gods. If that didn't seal their fate, my final innovation will usher in an irreversible evolution not just for theist holdouts but for all of the planet.

Where I was born and the mundane details of my early life are of little significance. However, the initial thrusts towards the biomechanical revolution started at University. Before my work came to be the building blocks of civilization itself, we still lived in urban sprawls of cold concrete and steel. A fetid waste pit of smog and filth. At that time the field of science was still awkwardly attempting to breakthrough into hyperreality with what they called "Dreamware". Cybernetic implants designed to integrate virtual space with the quackery of "consciousness". A fantastical concept of man's brain having a metaphysical element first expounded upon by phenomenologists of previous centuries. I've always found philosophy to be a masturbatory fiction of those with no other applicable skills. Nonetheless, I was forced into these dull minded experiments. Developing and building these foul little contraptions for hours on end. Soldering, aligning and staring through the magniscope until my eyes strained. Handling these microchips and circuits of silicone and metal disgusted me. I did not fathom the reason yet but I had an innate and visceral revulsion at these inorganic pieces of scrap.

The results of this series of experimentation were fruitless at best and catastrophic at worst, frying the subject's mind leaving them a drooling retard. I pontificated on how wasting such a powerful component like the brain in favor of toyish "Dreamware" was the exact folly that kept man in this cycle of utter failure. A cycle that needed to be shattered into thousands of unrecognizable shards. The most important lesson from this "Dreamware" debacle was about the ethics of science or lack thereof. Each of the subjects who met a painful end at the hands of these fools were shipped to the cryochamber. Their deaths covered up by university administration and their bodies filed away to hide their crimes. Despite these accidents, the experiments continued. The allure of profit and glory for a scientific breakthrough were well worth the pile of corpses left in its wake. The dean and faculty couldn't wait to pocket the checks that poured in from corporate interests.

Regardless I pressed on with my pursuits staying in the laboratory long into the night. The frozen corpses of deceased subjects made for optimal resource harvesting. My first innovation in biomechanics was an articulating arm. I clumsily sawed the appendage from the subject and fastened it to a base. I then used oscillating electric shocks to stimulate the muscles. At first it was unwieldy with involuntary jerks and spasms. But over time I perfected it, producing a controlled appendage with the capacity of fine articulation. My obstacle was the onset of putrefaction. After several days each arm would begin emitting a foul stench making it impossible to conceal even while frozen. I then developed my first revitalization serum from stem cells and vitamin extracts. This prolonged their use but nowhere near the longevity of living flesh.

I then shifted my focus to cloning of organisms in order to maintain a fresh supply of appendages for my innovations. Various rodents and reptiles were the limit of what was available as cloning of humans was still considered unethical by bureaucratic gatekeepers and their faux moral kennings. One evening I was outraged to find my idiot dorm cohabitator was rifling through my belongings. Despite my efforts to keep my notes cryptic, he managed to decipher enough to conclude that I performed successful cloning procedures. Impressed by my prowess he continued to pry into my work. Unwilling to reveal my intention I kept my answers jovial and vague. I was unsure if he was even capable of even replicating my studies, the thought of my work being plagiarized by some slack jawed yokel was nauseating. During our conversation he made a salacious suggestion in jest that came off absurd but later became a pivotal machination in the trajectory of my destiny.

What this dullard proposed was I extract genetic samples from a female professor that he found fetching so I could then replicate her for his pleasure. Although vacuous, this scheme seemed advantageous. Being an exclusive academic institution meant there was no shortage of bourgeois goobers willing to piss away their inheritance to satiate their carnal hunger. I managed to harvest enough samples in her absence that proved adequate for genetic replication. My first attempt was successful but being unfamiliar with the minutiae of human gestation, I only managed to create an infant clone. Although a perfect replica, this infant was not conducive for my purpose. So, I harvested ample tissue for more procedures and terminated it. To avoid possible consequences, I disposed of the remaining subject into the rat enclosure with expectations that they would devour any remains. I was correct in this assumption.

Later I developed adequate gestational facilities to ensure a clone could be grown to adulthood. To maximize efficiency, I performed gene therapy to accelerate the growth of the subject. This would result in a more manageable production speed. Once again, my assumptions were correct and my experiments were once again a success. The males within my dormitory were ecstatic at my newest innovation. Although wildly profitable, the cloned subject had little mental faculties and found her use traumatic. After some time the men found her mental state undesirable and her behavior became more erratic. To avoid detection I terminated her and again disposed of the subject in the vermin enclosure. To avoid this problematic outcome again, I performed another series of gene therapy to reduce the functionality of the frontal lobe among other neurological adjustments. This concluded in a much more docile clone acclimated specifically for the purpose of repetitious sexual use.

. . .

The accelerated growth carried into rapid aging as well. The adult replica had roughly 5 months in her peak form before beginning to age and becoming less desirable. At this point I would terminate the subject and harvest it for resources to carry out my biomechanical innovations. This model of seamless vertical integration made for optimal production of both funding and organic material. After several years without obstacles the administration caught wind of my activities through the electronic means that I managed my wealth. I was expelled from the university for breaking the rules that they so willingly ignored years prior. In exchange for my wealth, I offered to not expose them to the authorities for their Dreamware conspiracy. An offer they accepted and an offer I later reneged. For their hypocrisy I relinquished to federal agencies copies of evidence that I kept an immaculate account of. The Dreamware scandal was a media circus that resulted in multiple arrests and executions. No retaliation against me ever occured.

Using my model of profit and production with clones of famous actresses and performers, I managed to construct a laboratory that dwarfed the facilities I used previously. As time passed my innovations became more and more sophisticated. I eventually automated much of my operations with articulating limbs and various other organic apparatuses. Until once again I unfurled possibly my most potent discovery. "Orgrowth" or as the plebeians have aptly dubbed it "skin moss". A self maintained organic spatial cover that expands and heals, subsuming any rogue appendages in its fleshy network. I spliced human flesh with genetic matter from fungal growth to create a building material that transforms entire buildings into living structures that cost nothing and never need repaired. Under their superficial growth forms various nervous systems and sinews that emulate the function of power lines, plumbing and closed circuit networks. Networks that branch out towards each other connecting on their own volition.

This allowed me to introduce ever more sophisticated organic biomechanics. Arms, limbs and appendages that articulate and perform basic tasks. Eyes and ears that act as surveillance and communication biotech. Nasal organs and lungs to detect noxious fumes and purify the air from centuries of pollution. Orgrowth is both a civilizational and ecological marvel. Now entire urban centers are constructed entirely from enamel and orgrowth. Articulating arms aid the elderly, automate all labor and the collapse of industry has made for a cleaner more ethical human existence in harmony with nature. The introduction of brains into the orgrowth infrastructure has made our living cities even more efficient as all things are calculated, organized and carried out without the meddling of humanity.

My final innovation will usher in a new age. Yet another transformative evolution towards the end goal of the biomechanical revolution. Not just for a single city, technology or even just humanity but for the entirety of the planet. My final innovation is to integrate myself into the orgrowth superstructure as it spreads to eventually cover every inch of Earth's surface. The biomechanical network will be at the command of a central mind. My mind. As it was always supposed to be. The earth will be my body, an unfathomable organic amalgamate of millions of appendages, eyes and ears controlling all of the planet in harmonious unity. This is the final nail in the coffin for the technophiles and transhumanists. There is only to be one man to ascend to Godhood. My organic apotheosis is the finale of the biomechanical revolution. Through my genius I have made their science obsolete, their industry obsolete, their philosophies and morals obsolete.

Now the biomechanical revolution has made the totality of humanity obsolete.

Welcome
Introduction to The Bizarchives Issue #1

You stop in awe before the huge wooden double doors before you. Deep cherry wood adorned with otherworldly decorative filigree that seem to dance with haunting sway as you angle your head for deeper inspection. You are unsure how you've arrived here but any hesitation has been long dissolved by a ghostly siren song. An inaudible lullaby from some murky subconscious dimension gnawing at your mind, calling you here. You have never been here but you know in the depths of your being that you've always wanted this.

You lust for what lies behind this threshold. The very idea of turning back is unbearable. Unspeakable. It crawls under your skin like thousands of frantic spiders scurrying up and down your spinal cord. Jitters. Pins and needles. Short, shallow breaths and burning, itchy sweat. You run your fingers along the swirling engravings of the deep red doors as if you were caressing the body of a world class harlot. Riveted in the middle where the doors crease are two rectangular bronze plates etched with hand-shaped glyphs. Within the palms, various angular geometric shapes that emit a strange red glow as energy traces the etched lines like an arcane circuit board.

Enough. The world has given you nothing but boredom. Your entire stale, sterile existence of wage-slaving and hollow social etiquettes pale in comparison to this very moment. You firmly place your palms upon the bronze plates. A creeping chill travels up your arms and permeates through the entirety of your being. Such ecstasy. The heavy doors moan as they slowly swing ajar revealing a blinding kaleidoscopic glow of maddening hues.

Speechless, you numbly trapse into a confusing chamber of ghastly wonders. What vaguely resembles an immense library but disjointed and grotesque. Shifting walls of wood and stone schizophrenically assembled and stretching up to an obscured darkness, like an inverted bottomless pit. Towering cases chaotically stuffed with an uncountable array of tomes and scrolls. In every wall recess stands colossal marble statues of humanoid entities but twisted and bestial. Perhaps beings from far flung realms on the outskirts of reality.

This place shatters the very concept of sanity. It is a euphoric nightmare. The very manifestation of a million fragmented dreams constructed by a million deranged architects. Your senses polluted by a chorused confusion of flashes and hums of scattered oddities and artefacts that blur the line between magic and machine.

. . .

WELCOME

"We've been expecting you" a gravely baritone voice cuts through the commotion as the doors slam shut behind you.

Your eyes fix on a very tall, robed figure standing a few yards away. You're unsure whether he just appeared or if you simply didn't notice him in your awestruck stupor.

"You've been on your way here for a very long time." He says as he lifts a jeweled chalice to his lips. His long white hair and beard draped over lavish red and black priest-like robes.

You open your mouth but before you can ask he replies "This place contains all knowledge from places unseen and unknown. Knowledge that must be locked away. But you, you may now read it all to your heart's content."

The man smirks and continues "And for this reason, you may never leave. This is now your prison.."

"Welcome to The Bizarchives"

The Silver Key
Introduction to The Bizarchives Issue #2

The conceptualization of time itself has decayed. It has become inconceivable. You have no means of measuring how long you've haunted The Bizarchives and its countless wonders. One after another, you pull tomes from their perches and feverishly read them to their completion with no cognizance of day, week, or year. There is neither sun nor moonlight here. Only the dancing hues of numerous artefacts and oddities and a bottomless looming darkness above you. But never have you been stricken with fear or homesickness. Nor have you stopped to consider anything beyond satiating your newfound hunger for this knowledge.

"Here," the voice of the mysterious man startles you. You turn to see in his palms a peculiar obsidian box engraved with oblong eyes and tentacles that blink and writhe as if they were living. Within the box a silken lining of off-green. Nested in the box lies a tarnished silver key. Queer but ornate in design. The haft twists and swirls with an ophidian quality. The butt an intriguing but indiscernible mashing of symbols into a nimbus-like shape.

"What is this?" you ask with obsessive gaze.

The man smirks, "This is our most cherished artefact. It unlocks a gateway to the Mysterium, the dreamsea. A realm of imagination and wonder."

You reach into the box and grip the key with your fingers. Cool to the touch but not abnormal. You lift it to your eyes for intimate inspection.

"How did you get this?" you inquire

"Long ago, there was a man of incredible brilliance. He envisioned worlds of great wonder and told tales of terrible beings. Through his prose he gave others a glimpse into the dreamsea. In life he was the silver key. Now we hold but a manifestation of it. It was a gift from him to us," he explains

You ponder for a moment and reply, "But how can there be a realm of dreams when dreams aren't real?"

The man pulls back his hood to reveal his flowing silver hair as it falls down the back of his robes. "Real. What is real? Allow me to ask you this. In your world there are deep ocean trenches filled with creatures never seen by the human eye. Ask the common people to draw an image of one of these creatures and they will be unable to do so. It might as well not exist. Then ask them to draw a dragon and you will then have a pile of sketches depicting winged reptiles breathing fire. Which is more real? The unknown creature of material quality or the completely conceptualized immaterial creature?"

He continues, "This is why you're here. Why you've sought this place. In your world they have scoffed at the imaginative. Every child has their inspiration methodically cut from their souls as if it were a cancerous growth. Leaving a population of walking corpses with no hope nor vision. You've built a prison around yourselves where the only truth is material and the only accepted thoughts are increasingly meaningless abstractions. Your world has been sterilized by science. And to fill the void, they participate in more and more masochism. They have no heroes, no true innovations and no forward-thrusting spirit. Stagnant insectoids numbing their intellects with narcotics and screens. But as long as this key exists, those who desire it may remember how to dream."

You lift the key into the air as if to plunge it into some phantom lock. A phantasmal force guides your motions without your consent. Where you imagine the key should be inserted, an ethereal ripple travels outward with a humming wobble sound. From the point of the key, shimmering gold traces shoot out and rapidly cast the outline of a large arched door. Within moments, the outline fills itself with the translucent visage of a wondrous gateway. A shining golden door adorned with a blinding array of glitter and gemstones. Engraved upon its front, masterful depictions of mythic creatures and stunning constellations. As the ripple dissipates, the door manifests fully into a semi-material form still maintaining a ghost-like lucidity. An illuminating bluish mist slowly obscures your surroundings. A crank of the key cuts loose an echoing click. By its own volition, the door heavily swings awide.

Your eyes are forced shut by a blinding sheen as what lies behind the door is revealed. You are enchanted by a strong breeze that briskly howls into the room. It refreshes you, yet it has no discernable coolness or warmth. It blows, yet your hair and clothes remain still. You experience its delightful sensations, yet no effect can be observed. It is both real and unreal. Surreal perhaps. As your eyes adjust what unfurls before you as you stand at the threshold is a sight undreamed of. Stimulating so intensely that tears of sadness cascade to smiling lips. Laughter, fear, grief all liberate themselves at once for a schizophrenic cacophony of saccharine primality.

Beyond the door, an immeasurable landscape passes beneath you as if you were surveying a wondrous planetscape from atop a flying carpet. Herculean mountain ranges with crystalline snow tops. Puffs of icy powder trail from shards of rock faces as they dislodge and tumble. The peaks circled by majestic winged beasts unleashing echoing shrieks from their long fearsome beaks. Beyond the mountains, a vast featureless chasm of volcanic rock. Melting boulders helplessly drift down crawling rivers of lava. Far larger than any earthbound river and too numerous to count. From the jagged cliff edges of obsidian glass, the molten orange oozes and plummets to the chasm depths. Only a distant orange glow is visible beneath the dense toxic fog of sulphuric steam. Rumbling geysers burp forth poisonous gas and tectonic innards.

The black rock morphs into lush grasslands where magnificent docile creatures graze. Thick tufts of orange-brown shag dangle from their hides as they lean to their back legs using long articulating fingers to grasp pearlescent fruits from the tops of towering fungi. The earth quakes as the gargantuan grazers set their massive front limbs back onto the ground. In the distance upon sandy plateaus stand marvelous palaces of silver and ivory. Stained glass dome roofs display heroic ballads of ages yet to come and never were. Pristine marble corridors haunted only by the whistling whisper of gentle wind. A lavish royal chamber holding an empty throne with no heir nor claimant in sight. From the castle a blanketing, unending forest. Raw and primordial. Powerful trees, millennia old shrouding all beneath in darkness. Slithering carnivorous vines seeking curious mammalian bipeds to feast. Thousands of gangly simian swingers travel from branch to branch among the vast forest canopy like a pod of dolphins leaping through an ocean of leafy green.

Finally, the world stops to give you a picturesque view of a serene sapphire seascape. A waning evening sun sinks behind the horizon. The waters begin to disturb as your ears are assaulted by a thunderous disjointed groan. The sun begins to bleed an eerie purple essence into its sphere casting a chthonic aura. The clouds blacken with toiling hate as they swirl typhonically. Your heart beats faster as the trumpeting groan rattles the earth and distorts into a ghastly choir of nightmarish pitch. The water roils as thousands of eelish appendages emerge from the waves in a pulsing, formless mass. Thousands of deranged voices pollute your mind. All spitting hateful curses in thousands of long-dead tongues. The maddening crescendo comes to a sudden silence as two titanic glowing red eyes appear just beneath the surface. Their stare punctures their way into the furthest depths of your consciousness, drinking your memories and tasting your fears. You feel as though you are being summoned into their abyssal glow. You want to just let go and tumble headfirst into the writhing mass and be subsumed by this terrible æonic being. You offer your mind as its chalice to relish in the nectar of your sanity.

SLAM the door swings shut, sending you to your back. The outlines rapidly retract as the glitter and gold of the wondrous door fade. The entire door soon vanishes, and the key clangs onto the floor, no longer being suspended. Your senses return as you desperately try to regain your breath.

"Wh..what was that?" you pant

The robed man pulls you to your feet. "The man from whom this key manifested wielded great power. Although, in life, only those who saw his brilliance could see. He had prophetic insight into your world and the consequences of its follies, though many today curse him for it. He used his sight into the dreamsea to inspire countless souls to reach into it themselves. Many of the tomes you read here were inspired by his magnificent imaginative capacity. He will never be named among those whom your world considers as genius. But he belongs there."

"So what was that monster?" you ask

"You see. The master of the silver key wanted more than anything to help men dream again. But his legacy was reaching deep into man's most primal emotion. Fear. And he left behind not dreams of mystical worlds but unforgettable nightmares that will haunt men until they are inevitably swallowed by the hungering void," he says as points to your pocket.

You reach into your pocket and pull out a tarnished silver key. An exact duplicate of the key you previously used. You hold it out in your palm and look upon its features.

"You experienced the magic of the dreamsea, and now you know that it is indeed real. Whenever one peers into its wonder and its terror they can never lose its inspiration. So they then have the key to share with others. And eventually man will remember what it is to be inspired. And on that day they will once again dream of heroes and innovations. They will build great marvels and perform great feats. It all starts with this key," the keeper says as he scoops up the first key from the floor and carefully places it into the box.

"And who was the master of the silver key? What was his name?" You ask

The wizard pulls his hood back over his head and a wide smirk cuts across his face.

"Howard. His name was Howard Phillips Lovecraft."

Lex and the Odd Village
From The Bizarchives Issue #2

"Oohh Lucious Lex" Swoons the voluptuous raven-haired maiden as she dismounts Lex's mighty frame and sinks back into the opposite side of the oblong bronze tub. Hot steam bellows from the soapy water, obscuring the woman's soft but angular features and seductive, almond-shaped blue eyes. She attempts to wipe away some of her running makeup while she slowly wraps her luscious red lips around a freshly lit cigarette and takes a deep puff.

"Now you're what they call a *real man*, Ser Lex," she arouses as she caresses Lex's inner thigh with her soft foot under the water.

"Yes. I am real. Unlike you," Lex responds sternly with an inquisitive glare. He stays motionless with his back leaned against the side of the tub, arms relaxed and partially draped over the tub walls. Beard and stringy brown hair drip with condensation as he slowly shifts into a more upright sitting position. The large bath is dwarfed by the sheer girth of Lex's mammoth physique.

"Are you saying what I do isn't real work?" The woman snarls as she abruptly flicks her cigarette in Lex's direction.

A rare smirk cracks on his steamy grimace, followed by a chuckle in his belly that does not disturb his still posture. You would assume a man with such a burly build and immense stature would be hamfisted and clumsy. Not Ser Lucious Lex. Despite his size and thickness, the man moves with grace, and his posture is always calculated. Never nervous or impulsive. Ser Lex seems to always be in a relaxed state, always focused with full awareness. If there ever is a time Lucious Lex feels fear or rage, not even an empath would sense it.

His smile melts back into a cold glare. His crow's eye squint until almost closed. "Enough games. How many of you are there?" He inquires calmly.

The woman's annoyed expression slowly turns to confused concern as she cautiously lifts her hands from the soapy water and begins to lift herself from the tub exposing her large supple breasts. "I don't know what that means, Ser Lex. But you're starting to sound cra-"

Lucious lunges with incredible reflexes like a viper from its coil and envelopes the woman's head in his massive grip. A split second of a scream is quickly muffled as Lex plunges her head to the bottom of the tub. Her legs thrash about in the air as she desperately claws aimlessly.

clung clung clung, the bronze tub reverberates with the muted banging of Lex rhythmically bludgeoning the woman's skull as she drowns. After several more minutes of struggle, the woman finally goes limp. An expulsion of a final breath leaks from her lungs and bubbles to the surface. Lex holds fast, allowing the final vestiges of life to fade with a few postmortem twitches. A greenish murk clouds the bathwater, as all of the woman's black hair detaches from her scalp and floats among the tub like tufts of seaweed. Lex hoists the woman's head from the water to inspect her face still firmly in his clutches. But staring back at him isn't the gorgeous bar room hussie he sexed moments prior. It is the lifeless face of a hairless alienoid creature. Pale white flesh stretches over an elongated ovular cranium with two bulbous black eyes and recessed nasal protrusion. Dark green blood leaks from its ebon-gummed toothless mouth.

Lex's gaze is broken by the cracking of the door being kicked in. A thin, swarthy man in a barkeep's apron comes charging into the lantern-lit and wood-paneled bathing room wielding an axe overhead. Lex leaps to his feet and hurls the shape shifter's corpse at his would-be assailant. The body awkwardly tumbles through the air and gets caught by the bite of the axe, and gets brought to the floor with the barkeep's downward chop severing its legs. The barkeep gets a firmer grip on the wooden handle to attempt to wiggle his axe from the floorboards. His effort is interrupted when he's struck across the jowls with a hard wet slap of severed leg meat. The barkeep tumbles backward into the wood-paneled wall with his arms up in a pugilistic defensive stance. Stabilized against the wall, he peers up to see a hulking, naked, and dripping wet Lex charge him, brandishing a freshly severed leg gripped around the ankle. In a frenzy of combination blows, Lex feverishly beats the barkeep. His pathetic attempts of blocking the makeshift leg-club prove useless as each strike from Lex knocks him off balance in a different direction.

Lex sways slightly to the side as a wide swing from a large meat cleaver whiffs past his face from his flank. A second assailant of eerily similar appearance cocks his arm back for another swing. Lex swiftly closes the gap before his attacker can commence a second slash. With a shoulder-lead bullrush, the still-nude Lucious violently smashes his helpless opponent against the wall to the back of him. The knife-wielding barkeep grunts with frustration as if he's being slowly crushed under the weight of a fallen auroch. He attempts to wiggle his knife hand free, but Lex immediately grips his wrist in full control. With three bruising smashes against the hardwood panel, the cleaver is knocked loose from its wielder's hand and clangs onto the stone floor with a metallic ring. The pinned barkeep winces and snarls as the hulking hero gets a full fistful of hair. With a quick wall bash against the back of the barkeep's head for good measure. Lex turns and hurls him in the opposite direction to go stumbling into the path of his compatriot now brandishing his axe freed from the floorboards. Both men collide into one another and clumsily topple to the floor.

Before either men could gain their bearings, the barebodied Lucious Lex looms above them, axe in hand. Lex rains down a butchering upon them before they even get a chance to react. A brief scream of horror is silenced by a vicious series of indiscriminate hacks spritzing dark green blood all over the wooden walls and stone floor. Mere seconds after death, the mangled corpses of the barkeeps begin twitching and writhing, shedding their hair and twisting into identical forms. Paleskinned androgynous humanoids with lidless night-black spherical eyes. Jaws droop, frozen in a ghastly expression inconceivable to even the most deranged human imagination. Even the calloused Lex pauses for a moment at the unholy appearance of the changeling's inhuman form.

"They still appear manlike. The infestation must be recent. If the lord issues inquisition now he may be able to cleanse them," Ser Lex mutters to himself as he rushes over and attempts to bolt the door closed. The latching mechanism was obliterated by the first barkeep during his forced entry. Unclothed and in full flight, Lex quickly hops into his trousers, steps into his boots, and throws his dulled mail shirt over his bare torso. Like hot stones he tosses the loose pieces of platemail into his travel pack and hoists it over his shoulder. Slinking to the doorway, Lex presses his shoulder against the frame to peer out into the lantern-lit hallway. In the doorway directly adjacent to the washroom hangs a thick woolen curtain from a nailed in pig-iron rod. Lex leans his head into the doorway for a clear view into the room. He sees a moderately sized bunkroom of similar construction containing eight feather-stuffed beds with drab grey woolen blankets and worn wooden lockers at each foot. At the far end by the window, a chamberpot sits behind a makeshift privacy wall. The beds are all perfectly made and untouched. Not a soul to be found.

Lex does a swift exit maneuver from the room and begins down the hall towards the main tavern area, knees slightly bent. Each step falls softly like feline paws. Shield raised and mace tightly gripped. He leaves the short hallway to find a usually sparsely populated tavern strangely empty. The few round wooden tables and cherry-stained bar top are completely barren. Among the calm howl of the night breeze is the sound of flickering lantern flames and the slow drip of a leaky barrel tap being caught by a tin bucket. Ser Lucious creeps over to the bar to ensure no one lurks behind. All clear. All silent. He continues his way to the only feasible escape. The front door. With the front of his shield he pushes the door open.

Thunk th-thunk thunk

A series of crossbow bolts plunge into the warrior's heater shield, completely missing his bare hand. Across the dirt road a two wheeled farmer's cart is turned on its side. From behind it a posse of unidentifiable marksmen duck down to reload their projectiles. A pair of war cries emerge from Lex's flank. Two average-sized men dressed in full chain and crudely made basket helms come charging with polearms drawn. The first pike glances off Lex's shield, then immediately recoils. Before he can block the second strike Lex let's out a thunderous groan as two crossbow bolts tear through his flesh and lodge themselves in his muscular tissue, one in his upper thigh and the other in the lower back, thus leaving a brief window for a third pike stab straight by his shield and square into his guts. The wounded hero unleashes a roar of anguish as he falls to his knee. The two fighters make a final killing lunge to finish off Ser Lex. But at the final second he raises his shield forcing each pike to glance in his off-hand direction.

With a brief second wind Lucious drives his mace in a thrusting motion up under one of the attackers helmets, driving the point through his jaw and puncturing his brain. Following through with the stab motion, Lex side steps and pirouettes behind his second enemy, catching him in the crease of his elbow for a standing rear choke. Another folly of bolts pepper the pikemen in his torso, with the final one impaling Lex's forearm and penetrating into the man's jugular. Lex hooks his mace on his belt and reaches into a small leather pouch beneath his cloak. He pulls out a handful of small acorns. Lex utters a melodic incantation and hurls the enchanted nuts through the air. As the crossbowmen pop back up for another round of shots, the acorns land in a scattered grouping all about their covered location exploding on impact. The cluster of small explosions blow them to bloody chunks and launch singed innards and mangled meat through the air to splatter onto the dirt.

Hemorrhaging blood, Lex collapses onto the ground, barely conscious. Fifty paces away sits an open stable house. He begins to crawl towards it, bleeding profusely, coughing and gasping. Over scattered gore and fresh corpses he crawls, clawing at the dirt with every last bit of strength, dragging his injured limbs as they lose feeling and function. After the wretched struggle, Ser Lucious worms under the body of his acquired horse and pitifully rolls under a divider wall into a dark corner muddied by stagnant horse shit. He lifts his head peering down at his mutilated body from the only eye he's still strong enough to hold open.

Blood spits from his mouth with a morbid chuckle. Lex slides his arms inward and places his open palms upon his wounded torso. An eerie blue glow begins to emit from his hands as he whispers melodic hymns in the old divine tongue. Slowly the blue glow subsumes his entire form, swaying and pulsating with otherworldly translucence. Lex wheezes in discomfort as his body repairs itself. Ligaments rip and reform, tendons grow and shift. His gaping wound makes the revolting sound of moist sticky meat crawling into itself as the tissues bond together and mend. Two seperate clinks gently hit the stone next to him as the lodged crossbow bolts are pushed out by the healing muscular tissue rejecting the intruding matter.

Lex awakens to his boot being nudged by the opposite side of the divider wall. An abrasive beam of sunlight shines through a missing door plank forcing his eyes open. The horse nudges his boot again and loudly snorts bringing him to full consciousness. Groggy and disoriented, Lex rolls out from under the divider into a muggy, stinky horse stable. Using the trough as a crutch he brings himself to his feet. A few stiff paces brings him over to peer through the missing plank. In full daylight, the town is bustling as usual. The scene of last night's brawl in full view. No blood, no signs of damage. Even the farmer's cart has been replaced with a nearly identical one.

"They had to've heard the explosions," Lex groans with a scrunched brow.

He drops his travel pack and digs out the pieces of plate mail. Quickly he snaps, ties, and fastens every plate into place. Armor properly donned, he throws his tattered mantled cloak over his head and slings his pack over his shoulder. Lex slides the stable door wide open with his horse's reins in hand. The dozens of workers and passerbys abruptly cease their tasks and conversations and in unison turn their heads towards Lex. In a brief moment of eerie silence, the entire town casts a detached, wide eyed stare at Lex. Their lips pursed into an awkward half smile. The moment passes, and all the villagers turn back to their respective doings, and the strange pause ends.

Lex briskly treks down the main dirt road of the town towards the lord's mansion. For the entire walk not a single villager, shopkeep, or guard even looks in his direction, as if he was an unseen spectre floating through an ethereal veil between worlds. Eventually, Ser Lex approaches the lord's estate—a moderate two-story tudor of red stone and beige mortar. Sprawling vines of ivy climb the entire side of the house and reach out across several trellises to canopy a small cobblestone courtyard. An old, black iron fence surrounds the perimeter with a small gate at the front guarded by a single chain-adorned soldier.

As Lex approaches the gate to ask entry, the guard, without interaction or eye contact, unlocks the iron gate and swings it open. Hesitant, Lex ties his horse and cautiously approaches the guard.

"I am Ser Lucious Lex of the Tivarian order. I must speak with your Lord."

The guard cocks his head towards Lex. His is a suntanned broad face under a kettle helm. The same expression as the villagers earlier—a mindless distant stare and alien smile.

"Yes. Please come inside," the guardsman says with an odd cheerfulness before turning his head back to looking straight ahead.

Lex carefully walks by the guard, never breaking his distrustful glare, but no other gestures are reciprocated. With his typical gaunt lumber, Lex makes his way up the cobblestone path hearing the gate latch behind him. No other movement can be seen on the property. No gardeners, housekeepers, or even playing children. Yet the estate is in pristine condition. The walkways are swept, and on either side are running flower beds with bright polychromatic petunias and begonias.

Lex climbs up the small case of stone steps to a pair of chestnut arched doors with black iron hardware. On the left side a polished bronze panel with the heraldry of a black unicorn embossed upon it. He grips the unlocked doors and pulls them open. Lex walks into a large voyeur room with painted marble floors and burning lantern sconces. From the stone walls hang various murals of noblemen and cases holding pieces of fine art. On the far side under a decorative silk canopy sits four ornate wooden chairs.

Perched in each are four immaculately dressed nobles of near identical features. Curly brown hair, fair skin and emerald green eyes. In the middle sits a father and his wife. On either side a child of similar age. One boy, one girl. The father and son are dressed in ruffled white tunics, pale green trousers, and white hose from knee to buckled black shoes. The wife and daughter are adorned in ankle-length linen skirts with sky-blue blouses. Both wear matching pearl necklaces and amber earrings. Their curly chestnut hair laying down behind their ears.

As Lex approaches, the four nobles in unison train their odd stare on his movement as he comes into earshot. In each of their unique voices, but in perfect chorus they speak, "Ser Lucious Lex. I am ever astounded at your talent to escape death. I hope your lodging accommodations were to your liking. You must be accustomed to being among piss and shit."

Lex raises his mace "I'm going to kill every last one of you changeling fiends." He growls, gritting his teeth.

In uncanny harmony, the four nobles raise their palms. "And get the reputation for murdering a noble family? I think not. Go right along causing mayhem if you'd like. It's your standard forté," they choir.

"Mayhem?! You creatures create mayhem!" Lex refutes.

Lowering their hands they maintain their blank stare and emotionless half-smile "Fiends, changelings, creatures. What colorful monikers you pathetic men conjure to justify your fear. You presuppose a plurality here, because man cannot fathom a unified state of order. By his nature, humanity in his primeval multiplicity creates only chaos."

Lex takes a few steps closer, brandishing his mace ready to strike at any moment. "What happened to the dead changelings last night? Why just let me waltz in here?" Lex asks.

"Cleaned up. It's bad for appearances to allow a monster such as you to continue quenching your thirst for carnage. Why play in your court when you have no leverage? We simply needed to pacify you" the noblemen eerily reply in ghoulish ensemble.

"I'm a monster? You fiends are a race of parasites that kill and steal the forms of men," Lex retorts.

"There you are again, incapable of wrapping your feeble intellect around the very idea of unity. Man is incapable of true peace. We are nature's desperate grasp at establishing order through singularity. We don't have ego; we don't have rogue desires. We don't go traipsing around Grimeorth looking for wanton slaughter. That woman you murdered in the tub. What if your intuition was wrong and you just drowned some poor harlot? Would you feel remorse? Have you felt remorse for any of the innocent lives you've taken by mistake? No, you chalk them up to justified casualties. But the truth of the matter is you just kill by nature. You're a menace just like your father," the noblemen speak coldly.

Lex whiffs his mace through the air in frustration "I'll kill you for speaking of my father! You know nothing about him!" Lex shouts.

"We know everything about your father and his father and his father before him. Since our descent from the Dreamsea, we've observed man since his knuckles dragged in the dirt. Time and time again you apes rise and fall, never learning from your follies, repeating the same pathetic ego-driven atrocities. There is no me or I to kill, Ser Lex. We are woven into the very fabric of physical nature itself. From the most diminutive to the large, any organism that carries our blood is subsumed into the beauty of our harmonization. And one day all living things will be replicated and replaced, creating balance forevermore," they explain without ever changing emotion.

Lex slowly lowers his mace as his face turns to bewildered concern. "From the Dreamsea? So the lore is true. Changelings are commanded by the mindsoul. Why not kill and replicate me?" Lex inquires.

"Because unfortunately for you, Ser Lex, lineages such as yours cannot be assimilated into the harmony. And killing you would cost too much precious life. Besides, there is no institution capable of meddling in our expansion. Consider it silent justice allowing you to live the rest of your life knowing you can do nothing until you inevitably die in a scuffle with some hungry beast," they respond coldly.

"Lineages such as mine?" Lex asks with mace and shield loosely dangling at his sides.

"You had to have figured by now that your lineage had something special about it. But you're too stupid to ever uncover it. Now go. Leave us and never return. If you decide to go on a rampage, we will run and scream. Then your precious reputation as a hero will be sullied and you'll be known for the rest of your days as the bloodthirsty monster you truly are. Now go," the four nobles say in cold collective refrain as they each lift a pointed finger towards the opened mansion doors.

Lex glares at the hive-minded noblemen puppets for a few more moments before turning and storming out the doors, down the path, and out the gates. He unties his horse and begins leading it by the reins to the outskirts of town, passing by houses and workshops where villagers don't even acknowledge his presence. Lex's usual determined scowl is replaced by a lost, defeated gaze. At the town limits before the road winds off into rolling hills of grasslands, is a small storage shed stacked with bags of grain. At the corner, a small crowd of rats feeds upon a loose, open bag of grain. Lex reaches down and swiftly snatches a rat as they all scatter.

"Yes, friend. You may be right. Wherever I come from, whatever I am, I may be a monster. But I am mankind's monster."

Lex lifts the rat cupped in his massive palms to his mouth. He mutters a few terrible incantations of a blasphemous tongue and blows between his fingers onto the rat. The rodent twitches and squeaks in pain as its body bloats. Its skin twists and grows, open lesions oozing with yellow puss.

"And you speak truth, fiend. You would suffer many losses trying to slay me in battle. A battle I would surely lose. But even a monster such as I can't compete with the corpses piled by hands of lady plague."

Lex leans down and frees the sickened rat. As he mounts his horse and gallops off, the diseased vermin scurries through the nooks and narrows of the homes and workshops and into the heart of the village.

Lex and the Horror of Bernwick Hollows
From The Bizarchives Issue #2

The town of Bernwick. A sultry valley borough nestled betwixt the rolling bosoms of the Valelands. A commonly traversed resting place for weary travelers who prefer trekking the midlands instead of faring the treacherous waters of the black coast. Although its natives are quite hospitable, Bernwick is no stranger to its share of scandal. While most who frequent the unmarked roads of Grimeorth are purveyors of merchantry, the lawless wanders and wilds attract derelicts of subhuman instinct. The deranged and deviant oft slither their way into quaint communities such as Bernwick to quench their vile thirsts, only to slink back into the desolate mists to live among the unholy wraiths and hungering monstrosities that lurk throughout this cursed realm.

Lex halts his steed just before the town gate as the baking evening sun descends behind the stabbing ebon peaks of the distant trollspine mountains. He dismounts behind a small two-wheeled cart as its driver passes by a single guarding spearman in a studded leather hauberk. Lex approaches with reins in hand. After a quick investigative glance from the guard, he nods to signal him through. Like most settlements that dot these lands, Bernwick appears tediously ordinary. A main cobblestone street splits through its entirety with various stands, storefronts, and inns lined along it. Behind them clusters of erratically placed residential cottages of humble construction. Earthen plaster and stone with thatched roofs and bellowing chimneys casting grey puffs into the lingering smog above.

As the humid evening wanes, a cool night breeze ushers out the wafting aromas from the kitchens and cookeries as the shopkeepers and standing merchants lock up for the evening. Every corner and tavern stoop is populated by small gaggles of patrons and locals mingling with pints in hand. The choiring chatter and conversations occasionally interrupted by a boisterous outburst of some drunken chucklehead with his boots propped up. The stern-faced Lex cracks a smile, entertained by the carefree jubilance of inebriated yokels. Among the colorful chorus of unwinding townfolk, Lex hears the faint sobs of a nearby woman. He turns his head to see the cart that passed through before him at the gates, parked behind a nearby building. He approaches to see its driver, a young woman wrapped in a pale blue hooded cloak still perched on the front-facing bench. Leaned forward near collapsing in defeat, with her face buried in her palms. Her whispered cries indiscernible, muffled by her tear-soaked sleeves.

"What misfortune bewitches you, m'lady?" Lex inquires with baritone conviction.

Startled, the girl abruptly sits straight, quickly wiping her face with her sleeve. She replies with a poorly composed tone avoiding eye contact. "Good sir, I am in no need of wares or service. I am simply having a moment of grief. Now please, be on your way."

"I am no seller of wares, young one. I am called Ser Lucious Lex. I am a slayer of fiends, and I offer my aid at no cost. If my skills may be of help to you, ask one of the innkeepers. I doubt my presence will go unnoticed." He pats the edge of the cart's driver bench and turns to leave.

"Wait."

Lex turns back to face the woman as she halts his departure.

"Follow me to my family's inn. We've been closed for a few weeks but still have soft beds and provisions enough for a hot meal."

Ser Lucious nods and gestures for the woman to lead forth. The cart moves slowly as it bumps and creaks on the uneven cobblestone road. At the end of the main way, tucked back a few paces sits a terrifically crafted two-story stonework building. On one side a storehouse, the other an empty stable. Hanging above the center sitting doorway of the inn swings an ornate rectangular sign that reads "Talbert's Bread and Brew." The girl climbs down from her cart and trots up to the main door to unlock it with a keyring concealed under her cloak. She approaches Lex's horse and grabs the reins from his hand.

"I unlocked the door for you, Ser Lex. Please go upstairs and find a room to your liking. After you bathe and dress I should have supper prepared for you. Please go, I'll stable your horse for you," she urges.

Lex bobbles his head in brief contemplation before releasing his stead into the maiden's care. Upon entry, Lex scans the dimly lit, empty establishment. Although modest, the tavern is impeccably furnished with cushioned stools, polished oak bar tops and a masterful stone hearth with a large antlered beast mounted above it. On the far side, a set of carpeted steps with smooth wooden rails lead up a staircase partially illuminated by dying lantern sconces. With a more than usual labored gaunt, Lex makes his way towards the bar and leans over. From behind he pulls out a brown decanter filled with some unnamed spirit. With a pop of the cork he tips the swill back and takes a deep chug. With a grunt and a strained gulp he grips the rails and struggles up the steps.

Lucious doffs his battered plate and faded cuirass placing them in a locker on top of his mail and gambeson. After closing the box he hears a rap at the door. Lex turns the knob and pulls it ajar.

"Hot water for your basin, Ser Lex. I'll leave it here in the hallway. There's a hot stew on the stove and fresh bread in the oven. Come down when you're ready." The woman skirts off.

Lex fills his basin with the water and gives himself a warm wash. The heat soothes the countless scars and many physical malformations all over his brutish physique. He stands two heads taller than the average man with a thick, bearish visage. But every move is nagged by a constant ache from his body being hopelessly broken, healed, and broken again. The only remedy for his constant pain being a frequent warm bath and stiff drink. His gift of healing magic comes at a price. Torn flesh, mangled innards and shattered bones unnaturally reassembled and reformed over and over becoming more gnarled and twisted with each healing. Few men, if any, could suffer such a tormentful existence. But what drives this man is not of this world. His soul was shaped upon an anvil of wrath and tempered in hateful hellfire burning with the calamitous rage of a thousand suns. Last of the last of the Tivarian Order. When men have nightmares, they see devils. When devils have nightmares, they see Lucious Lex.

An enchanting scent permeates into Lex's room as he finishes fastening his shirt and trousers. The hearty aroma of seasoned meat and hot yeast trigger a roiling rumble in his neglected stomach. As if he's being summoned by a siren's song, the freshened warrior descends down the stairs into the empty dining area. On a roundtop table in the middle of the lit room sits a perfectly laid out dinner placement. Empty copper bowl with utensils, cloth napkin, and pitcher with ale froth foaming over the side. Lex sits and tips the pitcher to pour the golden ale into a pewter pint. He lifts his eyes to see the young woman come scampering in from a back room lugging a steaming iron pot. Lex pauses stricken by the form of the maiden he hadn't noticed before. Youthful and rosy, her curly strawberry hair pulled back into tail. Earthy hazel eyes partially covered by curled bangs. Milky fair freckled skin and full pink lips upon her round face. A light flowing linen dress poorly concealing her voluptuous curves.

"My grandmother's recipe, Ser Lex. I pray that you enjoy" the girl scoops a wooden ladle into the creamy brown stew and fills her guest's bowl nearly to the brim. Lex fixates on her beautiful shifting physique as she scampers to the counter to bring over a metal plate with hot bread sliced and fanned out for proper display.

"All this is quite unnecessary, m'lady."

"Alora. Call me Alora. It is I who should be addressing you with titles," she assures as she sits down across from him.

"So, you've heard of me?" Lex asks with attention focused on blowing the steam from his spoonful of hot stew.

"Of course. Who hasn't heard the tales and rumors of Lucious Lex the slayer?" She waves her hands sarcastically.

"What of the rumors?" Lex halfway inquires with a mouthful of bread.

"That you were born of beast and your presence is known by the stench of death"

"And what is your impression of the beastman before you, Alora?" Lex smirks.

"Although you are much larger than I could have imagined, you seem human enough to me. But the second part is true.

Hence why I offered you a wash." Alora raises her brows with a smile. The two share a friendly chuckle.

"So, tell me Alora. How may I repay this wonderful hospitality?" Lex leans back as Alora fills his bowl and ale a second time.

"It's my brother and mother. They're missing. Since my older sister passed my mother has developed an obsession with brewing medicinal concoctions for any possible future sickness that my brother and I may catch. For this most recent salve she needed corvus root, a plant that only grows in caves. Less than a week ago she left to go find it. After she didn't come back, my brother left to go search for her. He hasn't come back either," she explains

"What about your father?" Lex inquires taking the last bites of bread.

"My father died before I was born. He fought in the last mongrel crusade. Both he and my grandfather were legion and fell during the massacre. They were named Talbert. The namesake of this tavern." Alora assumes a solemn frown.

"Heroes. My father fell then, too. I wear his armor. I'm the last of the Tivarian Order, the fraternity your family hails from as well. Your brother inherits this lineage," Lex says profoundly.

"My brother has a different father. My mother married the local baker. A drunk fool but left us with some wonderful recipes before he ran off with some harlot," she snarls.

"So what is this cave?" Lex asks.

"Bernwick Hollows. The locals say it's a portal to the demonic realms of Murkwood, and those who go in are dragged into the underworld by fiends. My mother said these were fool's tales from illiterate drunks and those who didn't return fell down into dark crevices. Either way, I just want my family to come home." Alora chokes as a few tears trickle down her rosy cheeks.

Lex wipes his face with the cloth napkin and stands up. "Draw me a map to the caverns, and place it here on the table. I will head there at first daylight." Lex takes his leave as Alora begins gathering the dishes. He climbs the steps back to his room for the night.

Before the morning sun crests Lex comes down the stairs donned in full armor. A fairly well drawn map sits on the cleaned table where he had eaten the night before. After a thorough examination he folds the map and sticks it into a belt pouch. In chilling morning air he unhooks his horse and rides off through the town at full gallop and down into the valley. Alora's map proved true. A few hours' ride and another hour's hike through the sparse pine forest lead Lex to the large dark cave mouth of Bernwick Hollows. After tying his stead to a nearby tree he descends within the damp cavern. With each step further into the subterranean hole the outer light becomes more faint, obscuring Lex's vision. Condensation cascading from jagged stalagmite tips drip into lonely puddles, casting ghostly echoes in the near distance. Every step becomes more treacherous upon the slimy rock and rubble beneath his feet as he trudges deeper into pitch black darkness.

With a whispered hymn he holds up his spiked mace, and it brightens with a heavenly iridescent glow. The trusty bludgeon illuminates his immediate vicinity to reveal much of the same chaotic cave features. Lex follows the corridor as it bends and winds down deeper into the hazy depths. Every so often he is startled by the echoes of scuttering taps from crawling legs. He waves his magic torch about scanning for predatory subsurface denizens, but the cave's reverberation makes locating near impossible. Every slithering shadow when illuminated reveals to be nothing. Lex takes a step down through a ridged threshold to see a bit of shining sunlight emblazing something astounding. He lurches closer, offhand maintaining balance on the coarse cave walls and steps into the light.

The near sounding of casual speech reaches his ears. Before him a large cavernous chamber brightened by sunlight. In the middle shimmers a serene pool of crystal water. As his eyes adjust, the chamber comes into full vision. A lavishly decorated alcove with stone walls and marble floors. Relaxing in the pool and wading about are beautiful women in scanty attire. All around, various furnishings and cushioned chairs where patrons enjoy decadent goblets of wine. Lex cautiously enters attempting to draw little attention. To his side a gathering of low sitting pillowed seats. Engrossed in them a few people casually dressed. He scoots to the chairs and leans down to a napping woman.

"Excuse me madam, I am searching for the owners of Talbert's Bread and Brew from Bernwick."

The woman continues to sleep undisturbed. Across from her the frail voice of a young man answers.

"My mother and I run Talbert's along with my sister Alora. Will she be here soon?" The dark haired boy replies. Upon further inspection the boy appears emaciated with sunken eyes.

"I am here on behalf of your sister, Alora. She asked me to fetch you and your mother. Is she here?" Lex asks with unease.

An older ginger woman in plain dress raises shaky fingers "Yes dear, I will be home soon. Alora needn't worry. It's been ages since I've enjoyed the shoreside. Especially one as pristine as this'n."

The boy chimes in "We've worked so hard since my father left. It's such a relief to enjoy being out in nature like this. No drunken oafs shouting, no bar fights. Just the mountain breeze."

Lex gets a puzzled sneer, "shoreside? mountain breeze?"

He slowly lowers his belly to the floor and covers his nose and mouth with his cloak. His sight blurs and distorts as the pool of relaxing maidens transforms into a ghastly murky pond with bobbing and bloated corpses. His surroundings morph back into the jagged cavescape. Hallucinatory furnishings reveal their true horrific appearance. A slimy cavern floor littered with scattered bones and shredded human remains. The chairs around the chamber, thick stringent webbing with deflated carcasses of animals and humans. Several of them are mounted by hideous arachnid creatures sucking the liquified guts from their torsos through a syringe-like tongue appendage. Lex turns to Alora's beloved family to see they are stuck to large webs, cocooned in slimy adhesive regurgitant.

Leaping to his feet, Lex begins to hack at the webs around them, jostling and freeing them from their oozy cells. In a numbed daze, the two don't even react to the disturbance. All around the chamber the creatures scurry out of every tunnel and crevice alerting, one another with an abominable chattering choir of clicks and gurgles. As Lex frees the pair, the dog-sized creatures descend upon him. Thorax of a lanky legged spider with numerous wispy sensory apparatuses. Bulbous pulsing abdomen housing a curved stinger oozing with milky toxin. Sprouting from the front of their bodies a dwarfed humanoid torso with two freakish bony jointed arms and three-pronged claw hands. Their heads, perversely manlike but spherical. Randomly dotted with countless unblinking insectoid eyes all across the front of their skulls. When these mockeries of nature close in to attack, their grotesque jaws unhinge to reveal a maw full of hooked fangs. Nightmarish, straw-like tongue that telescopes out to half their body length.

Lex finally frees both of Alora's kin but senses the leaping monster attempting to strike from behind. With his boot to its abdomen, Lex drives the creature to the stone, pinning its pulsing stinger. It snaps viciously and lunges its daggered tongue into the hero's chestplate only to ricochet off. With his gauntleted grip he tears the tongue from the monster's mouth. With incredible reflex he avoids the desperate bites and grabs hold of the fiend's black-skinned head. With foot anchoring the body, Lex twists and ratchets the foul cranium, tearing it from the body. The beast twitches and curls as it sprays yellow bug guts. A second arachnoid pounces stinger-first but clangs into the immoveable shield now in the firm grip of Lex's offhand. With a crushing downward swing, the warrior's mace collides with the creature's head, bursting it into yellow mush. A third drops from the ceiling, but Lex firmly holds his shield overhead. When the devil collides, Lex thrusts the monster to the side falling directly into a cave spike, impaling itself.

The battle continues with Lex swinging, smashing, and obliterating an uncountable number of these sinister monstrosities. Yet the onslaught grows ever fervent as hordes of the crawling horrors pour out from every cave orifice. He loudly chants the illumination hymn and his yellow stained mace flashes with blinding brilliance. The insurmountable throng of despicable man-spiders shriek in pain as they recoil from the searing divine light. Thousands of little clicks from their crawling steps congest the chamber's soundspace as they frantically attempt to scurry into holes away from the light. Lex holds his mace proudly as a deterrent as he scoops up the pair and hoists them onto his shoulder, one stacked upon the other. With a bull's strength, Ser Lucious stomps up through the threshold and into the corridor. He slips and skates, losing footing with every fifth step. At quarter speed the slayer summons all his might to escape the cave, but the scuttering crowd begins to follow suit. A chase ensues.

From every portal and crack the creatures poke their heads out as Lex passes through, but as his shining mace fills his vicinity with illumination, they recoil back. Just out of the reach of the light, hundreds of them blanket every surface of the cave from top to bottom. One false step, and the three of them will be torn to pieces. A grotesque feast for these hellish abominations. One drops down before Lex and launches its knife tongue appendage. Lex side steps to shield the rescued victims but the bladed tongue bypasses his plate and deeply slashes the underside of his bicep. It immediately recoils in full blaze of the burning light. It tries to shield its eyes, but Lex delivers a devastating horizontal blow, breaking its hands and pulverizing its squishy face. In the distance, the soft glow of evening sun breaks through the darkness. Lex cuts loose a roar of determination as he trudges forth, each exhausted step closer to salvation.

Finally, the winded hero emerges into the sunlight. On his heels the spiders stop in their tracks, seething and hissing in anguish scurrying back into the shadows of the cave. Lex lumbers over to his horse and slumps the two cocooned victims over his horse and unhooks its reins. Upon his stead he trots by the cave entrance. From the darkness, thousands of tiny and glowing red eyes peer out at him. He triumphantly holds up his mace that is no longer glowing. The horde flinches at the sight of the mace and collectively screech in disapproval. Lex gallops off with a smug grin.

Nightfall descends upon Talbert's Bread and Brew when a pound at the door alerts Alora from her seat. She rushes to the door and flings it open to see her missing family members standing in the doorway and leaning on one another as they come to their senses. Alora explodes into joyous tears as wraps them both in an ecstatic hug. She helps them inside and sits them down. Immediately after, Alora comes charging out to Lex mounted upon his horse in the middle of the street.

"I knew you could do it! Whoever speaks ill of you, may they suffer in Murkwood! You are a blessing from heaven, Ser Lucious Lex. The Gods sent you to us." She sobs into his leg as he straddles his horse.

He reaches down and peels her off of his boot "The tales about the cave were true. There are friends there. Far too numerous to slay. Explorers get subdued by poison air, and the monsters feast on them. Tell the locals to stay far away."

She takes a step back with palms clasped "You're bleeding. Why don't you stay another night and let me patch you up? I'm sure you'll find that my bed is far more comfortable."

Lex cocks his head staring off down the road. "M'lady Alora, you are an enchantress. However, if I left you with child there would be no possibility of you wedding a good husband. A husband you need to care for your family and business. I will return again for that wonderful stew. If you are unmarried and still hold your beauty, I will happily bed you. Farewell, Alora"

Tears stream down her rosy cheeks as Lex gallops off into the night.

"Farewell to you, too, Ser Lex… my guardian angel."

Alora wipes her tears away and turns to go back inside. After finishing up the last of the reheated stew Alora helps her disoriented brother and mother to their beds. She tucks them both in, squeezes them tightly, and kisses them on their foreheads. After putting out their lights she makes her way downstairs to lock up the doors and gather the dishes. Startled, she drops the dishes on the floor. She listens in horror at the sound of scuttering taps on the rooftop. Hundreds of glowing little red eyes peer through the windows from the darkness.

Lex and the Lost Girl
From The Bizarchives Issue #1

"*P**lease heeelp!*"

The forest's nightly silence is shattered by a young woman's desperate shriek. Her flowing red hair clinging to her sweaty skin as she frantically tries to pry the briars from her filthy linen dress. Tears streaming from her panicked eyes as her pursuer rapidly closes in. Sticks and brush crunch underfoot from the large galloping paws. Shallow hot breaths and snarls from a salivating bestial mouth becoming more frenzied with every nearing lurch.

"Ohh no-no-no please please no" the ginger girl's struggle quickly melts into sobbing defeat as she makes a few more pathetic jerks to free herself from her thorny prison.

. . .

Bursting through the brambles lunges a bipedal wolf-like monstrosity with it's long crocodilian jaws agape. The girl's scream of terror is interrupted as the beast snaps it's jaws around her torso and violently rips her from the briar bush. Bones crunch and flesh tears as the beast whips the helpless girl back and forth like a chew toy sinking it's fangs deeper. In seconds cries of pain become bloody gargles and convulsions. In a final jerk the monster swings it's head and tosses the mangled mess of a woman through the air to collide with a thick oak tree.

Her dress shredded and insides exposed, the torn girl uses her last bit of strength to force her eyes closed as blood pools all around her. Eyes glowing red the monster approaches, long forked tongue writhing between its hooked teeth to taste the morsels of freshly lodged meat. Blood spattered all over its black fur and spines that pepper down its slender back. Steaming drool drizzles from the creature's open jaws as it looms over its victim ready to finally feast.

Drunk with hunger the creature gets blindsided by a charging force. Taken off its feet and smashed into the large oak tree. Sandwiched by an oversized kite shield. Wielding it, an absolute mountain of a man. The beast frantically claws and bites out of desperation as his foe digs in his boots applying more and more pressure. The wolf demon yelps as it's bones crack behind the shield's force. It's desperate attacks doing nothing against the man's battered plate armor. Piss and shit begin to evacuate the fiend's bowels. The warrior steps back releasing the disoriented creature and with a tiger's reflex swings his mighty spiked mace. With crushing force the mace collides with the monster's head sending bits of skull and brains into the air like gruesome party favors.

The power of the man's swing sends the beast headfirst into the dirt. Before the creature's body even lands a second strike comes crashing down completely exploding its eye sockets. The demon's body twitches involuntarily as the hulking hero lands blow after blow completely obliterating its skull. Turning from the oozing mangled mess of a monster the man calmly walks over to his traveling pack a few steps away. After a bit of rummaging he pulls out an antique lantern. The artefacts black iron twirled into ornate designs. He pops open one of the small stained glass panels and reaches his robust fingers in to fiddle with the wick. From his pack he finds a match and sparks it on a nearby stone. The tiny match flame makes contact with the wick and the lantern glows with an unnaturally large illumination. The six glass panels on the lantern begin to slowly turn projecting the stained glass images on the surrounding trees.

The light reveals the man's visage. A powerful barrel chested form standing as tall as a brown bear. His broad shoulders hoisting a battered set of platemail. On the cuirass a faded insignia of what appears to have been a lion's head. Hanging from his back a tattered brown cloak that hangs just above his greaves which are fastened by bits of makeshift leather cord. The dancing light shines on his emotionless resting scowl. A large moon-shaped face with unkempt beard and healed scars from a thousand brutal fights. From under a protruding brow, a pair of dull hazel crow's eyes forever frozen in an expressionless stare. Partially hunched he walks with a slight limp.

. . .

The man carefully lumbers over to the girl's body and kneels down to feel for a pulse. *"She has seconds left"* the warrior whispers to himself as he hangs the curious lantern on a branch above the bloodied girl. He places both his hands gently upon her back and closes his eyes. A ghostly blue glow begins to emit from his palms as he purses his lips. The blue energy slowly travels over her entire body enveloping her. She twitches with a silent cough as her flesh begins to repair itself. She winces with a whimper with the cracking sound of bones realigning. The blue energy subsides and her eyes pop open with shock. Quickly the man's palm covers her mouth pressing the back of her head into the bloody mud.

"Quiet girl. Scream and there will be more." The man quietly warns.

She nods in agreement and he lifts his hand from her mouth. *"Am...am I alive?"* she whispers with quivering lips.

"Yes. I healed you. You've lost your beauty but you're alive. You will have pain from now on. But pain is better than death." He coldly mutters.

"You killed that creature? Who are you?" She asks.

"Yes. Tell me where you live. I will take you home" he replies.

. . .

"Before the northern hills, my family has a farm east of the blue spring." She explains as she slowly climbs to a crouch.

"Farm? Horse farm?" He inquires.

"No, we grow barley and squash but my brother keeps a horse to pull carts from the heath." She answers.

"Good." He affirms as he wraps his cloak around her revealed body. Grabbing her by her ankles and arms he tosses the girl over his shoulders like a suckling pig. The dark forest slowly starts getting lighter as the morning sun crests. With every brisk step the warrior surveys his surroundings with keen eyes.

"My name is Nissa, sir. Thank you for saving me." She says sprawled across those massive shoulders.

"You're welcome, Nissa. I am called Lucious" he replies with arms firmly securing Nissa's body as he continues through the woods.

Her eyes widen *"Lucious? As in Lucious Lex the slayer?"*

"Yes." He sternly replies.

. . .

"I can't wait to tell my brother. He's going to be so excited to meet you. So, you just run around killing monsters all day?" Nissa asks.

"Yes. Fiends prey on men. I prey on fiends. I am mankind's monster." Lex responds.

Nissa lifts her scarred lips for a warm smile as she reaches her arms around Lucious' forearm for a grateful hug. The pair stop at the exit of the woods to bask in the warmth of the full afternoon sun. The golden rolling hills before them bearing large swaths of swaying barley about ready for harvest. A long winding dirt path seperating two crops down the middle. At the top of the hill a thatched roof can been seen peering over the hill crest. Poking out, a cobblestone chimney bellowing a wispy cloud of pale grey smoke being guided crossways by a gentle summer breeze.

"I can walk from here" Nissa says as Lucious carefully lowers her to the ground. She holds onto him until her shaky legs finally find their footing. Nissa smiles and waves for him to follow her as she hobbles up the dirt path. The two make their way up the road and approach the humble farmstead. A standard clay block house with a large tool shed and small stable attached. Parked in front of the tool shed sits a small wooden cart with large spoked wheels yoked to a shabby but strong looking work horse. Leaving the shed with arms full of tools is a lean built young man with sandy hair and deep tan. Tarnished beige tunic tucked into brown trousers help up by a piece of rope. The young man stops immediately as soon as he locks eyes with Nissa in the near distance.

. . .

"Nissa?! I thought you were..." the young farmer drops all of his tools and launches full sprint to greet his sister. His jubilant gallop halts ten steps away and his face freezes in horror as he looks upon the healed scarring on his sister's disfigured body. His eyes turn from shock to rage as his gaze turns to Lex.

"Thom, settle dow-" before Nissa could finish her sentence her brother charges at Lex brandishing a long filet knife.

"What have you done to my sis-" with a thunderous crack Lex's mighty gauntleted fist crashes into Thom's face. His neck snaps backward as broken teeth and blood blow out from his mouth. The young man's unconscious body collapses unnaturally onto the dirt. *"Thom!"* Nissa rushes over to tend to her squirming brother and lifts his head. She looks up, alerted by the sound of jostling buckles and sees Lucious unhooking the workhorse.

"Sir Lex, what are you doing?! That's our only horse!" Nissa shouts

"Get another horse. I'm taking this one" he coldly states as he mounts the horse and trots by her. Thom and Nissa watch as he gallops off into the distance.

Lex Conquers Hell
From The Bizarchives Issue #3

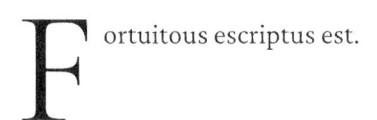

F ortuitous escriptus est.

"Begone, traveler, Lord Emeric isn't receiving visitors. His daughter has fallen ill," the stout guard barks at Lex from behind his kettle helm.

Lex peers up the lavish mansion wall, scanning for commotion through any of the windows.

"Fallen ill? I am no fool, sentryman, and judging by the fear in your eyes you know who I am," Lex growls, stabbing him with his gaze.

The guard makes a hard swallow and shifts uncomfortably, "Yes, y..you are the slayer Lucious Lex."

"If you do not open this door you will force me to break through it. And break through you."

The guard shudders nervously at the baritone rattle of Ser Lex's command. After a moment of anxious hesitation the guard scurries over to the door and twists the brass doorknob.

As it swings slightly ajar Lex grips the edge and rips it open, knocking the guard off his feet. Ser Lucious barrels through the doorway into a small foyer, dimly lit by several low burning lantern sconces. A red carpet with silver floral patterns lies centered in the aisleway, across an impeccably polished rosewood floor. Striped papered walls are adorned with various framed artworks, which all hang crookedly. The floors are littered with shattered porcelain, fallen from disturbed shelf perches.

Upon entering, Lex is startled by a monstrous tone resonating through the estate halls. The amplified scream of a young woman overlays with bestial roars of nightmarish quality, far louder than any human vocal cord could produce. The sconces flare up in unison with a scorching blood-red hue, blackening the ceilings above. The hellish orchestra of roaring flame and horrid pitched scream rattle the entire house as glass and ceramic smash all around. As the scream wanes and the sconces die down to a dim glow, a robed figure steps into view from the far staircase.

"I don't know why that idiot Norwyn let you in, but she doesn't want you here, Lex. No one does." The exhausted timbre of an emaciated figure struggles to reach Lex's ear. Accompanied by two guards with sheathed cutlasses, a frail looking middle-aged man lurches closer. Grey wispy hair sits upon an oval head with deep-set, brown eyes under a long angular brow. Thin chapped lips, gaunt, high-sitting cheekbones with unkempt evening scruff. Draped around his shoulders a large silk sleeping gown, deep blue with a gold lace hem. The garb completely conceals his figure like a fearful child swaddled in an oversized quilt.

"I heard you came here to Cliffmoor. You're here to kill my baby girl, Lex. Lex, the vigilante slayer," the man says mockingly with haughty inflection.

Lex slowly lowers his shield and fastens it to his back. "I've come to investigate rumors of trollish activity, Lord Emeric. Has your daughter been stricken?"

"Investigating the gossip of illiterate yokels? How lucrative that must be. Well, no such activity will be found here. Be on your way, slayer. My daughter needs an apothecary not an exorcism," Lord Emeric scoffs.

Lex trails his eyes across the floor at the shattered mess of glass and ceramic shards. "Never heard of black fever causing houses to shake or lanterns to flare," he argues.

"Coraline will return to health with the unbridled attention of her devotees. We are family here, and you will not meddle in our affairs. Do not test me Lex! Now piss off!" The man's glazed expression explodes into hateful obsession as he clenches his fists. Unfazed by the nobleman's outrage, Lex takes a step closer and continues his inquiry.

"Devotees? I'm going up to see Coraline for myself." He begins a straight line to the stairs. The two guardsmen charge, reaching to draw their cutlasses. With lightning precision Lex strikes the drawing shoulder of his first assailant as he reaches across his body to grip the cutlass pommel.

The guard screams in anguish as his bones crunch under Lex's mace. A prompt frontward snapkick from Lex's greaved shin lands squarely into his attacker's groin. He collapses to his knees clutching his pulverized nuggets with one hand as the other hand dangles uselessly from a destroyed rotator cuff. Lex spins to face the other henchman as a glancing slice bounces off his pauldron.

With the momentum of his turn, Lex follows through with a broad, horizontal swing. The spiked mace head collides with the swordsman's neck. Any bladed weapon would have sliced through the entirety of his neck, sending his head into flight. But the blunt force of Lex's strike disintegrated his vertebrae.

With a chilling squeaky gasp, the guard's skull flops awkwardly before he falls to the floor, twitching in his death throes.

Lord Emeric unleashes a frenzied scream, lunging with a ceremonial serpentine dagger drawn from under his gown. The jagged blade point breaks as the deranged nobleman foolishly attempts to plunge it into Lex's battered cuirass. Like a bear swinging its mighty paw, Ser Lucious delivers a backhanded swipe. Emeric's frail frame is sent flying sideways to crash into a tall curio cabinet. The glass panel doors and porcelain wares shatter. Shards of glass tumble down on him as he crawls about on the floor groaning in frustration.

"How...how dare you put hands on me! You putrid derelict! I'll cut your throat myself!" the bloodied lord protests as he squirms about in a nest of glass and splintered wood.

"Cripples can't fight," Lex says in a frigid tone as he presses his boot down upon the lord's lower back. With baneful frenzy, Lex delivers blow after blow of downward strikes, brutalizing his shins and knees. Emeric wails in agony as his nails break upon the rosewood floor panels he claws in desperation. Lex steps off and makes his way toward the far staircase. The lord, fraught with hateful sobs, rolls himself onto his back. His mangled leg meat flops and folds in unnatural ways as if no bone was there to give form.

"Th..there will be no help for you Lex. I will have you tossed from Cliffmoor's crags and laugh as y..you dr..drown in the ocean," Emeric curses beneath his labored cries.

Another demonic howl rumbles the stairs beneath Lex's feet as he climbs to the second floor. Harrowing ethereal whispers cloud Lex's mind, repeating, "he... arrives... he arrives... he he arrives... he arrives arrives... he arrives..."

The sconces on the stairwell begin to glow a gloomy crimson, illuminating the stairwell in a grim aura. The ghostly murmurs cease abruptly as Lex takes a final step onto the second floor landing. The thick air stands still in chilling silence. At the end of the hall, a single door cracks slightly ajar, casting an eerie sanguine phosphorescence into the hallway. Droning groans of wheezing breath bellow from the room as a creeping stench of putrefaction pollutes the air.

In a cautious prowl Lex approaches, brandishing mace and shield firmly in his grip. The unsettling groan stops as the lurking hero moves his shield to nudge the door open. Before it makes contact, the door swings open by its own volition to reveal a scene too unspeakably grotesque for common eyes.

In this disheveled bedroom, torn walls are spattered with blood -- smeared into unholy shapes and sigils. Slumped all around lie the mutilated carcasses of a dozen victims. Men, women, children, all dismembered and intentionally placed like some grotesque art display. At the foot of the bed stands an ominous obsidian altar of deviant construction. Carved into its precipice, an abhorrent angular symbol. Skewed and star-like with six points that beckons into his mind, insinuating horrors of some untold nether realm.

"Leeeeexxx," a horrid groan spews forth from a feminine figure as it arches its spine and bends its torso to align with its already vertical legs. Now standing on the bed, it stares at him as its head turns and twists with the cracking and shifting of bone. Pink drool leaks from a pitch black mouth of broken teeth chewing on a lacerated tongue. Milky pupilless eyes ooze from their deep-set swollen sockets. Matted black hair dangles sparsely from a scalp dotted with open sores and infected lesions.

"Speak your name, demon," Lex commands.

The woman's body lowers its head ghoulishly.

"Yaotzn'lek," it drawls with an open-mouthed groan.

Lex pauses with determined eyes, awaiting its strike.

"Pathetic... your antiquated formulas of banishment have

always been old wives' tales," the demon mocks. "Now come, warrior. Put this bitch down and release me. I hunger for a new vessel. Unless..."

The woman's body thrashes about violently and thrusts itself onto its back. Bestial snarls fade into the sensual hot breaths of a woman's voice. She sits up and all ugliness has vanished, a beautiful woman with torn nightwear revealing her luscious breast.

"Unless you want to take me first?" she moans as she lifts her gown and spreads her legs to show him her bare slit. Her hips gyrate with anticipation as she beckons Lex with orgasmic purrs.

"This is what you came for isn't it, hero? To save me and to bed me. You go from town to town touting some code of righteousness. But it's all so you can spit your rotten seed into the cunts of these stupid whores. Ooohh Lex, why do you tease me? Take me now."

Lex hangs his mace on his frog hook and approaches with shield lowered. The woman seductively crawls to the bedside licking her puffy red lips. Lex stands before her as she peers up with hungry blue eyes.

"Am I speaking with Coraline now?" He questions.

"Yes, my love. It's just us here." She runs her palms up his thighs and begins to unfasten his belt.

"May you find peace."

A pair of silver manacles latch themselves around her wrists. The woman looks up in rage as an upward knee strike sends her body tumbling backward onto the mattress. The beauty melts away instantly transforming back into her previous ghastly form. The demon roars as a magic cord emerges from the cuffs and wraps itself around the entirety of Coraline's body from shoulder to ankle.

"What trick is this?!" the possessed girl demands.

"An artefact uncovered from an antediluvian temple. It binds extraplanar entities, as you can see. They're called devils' shackles," Lex explains as he fixes his belt and draws his mace.

Helpless, the demon spreads a black smile as Lex's mace smashes square between its eyes. The nasal cavity collapses as Lex follows with several more mashing thuds sending pink matter into the air. Coraline's corpse lies motionless as the devil's shackles unbind and fall off her wrists.

Lex scoops them up and fixes them to the back of his cloak's hidden belt. With a few mighty whacks, Lord Emeric's profane black stone altar is broken into unrecognizable bits. Upon exiting, Lex finds that Emeric and his remaining guard have fled, leaving a blood trail from the Lord's wounds.

Walking through the house Lex dislodges the lanterns from their sconces and tosses them onto the floor, engulfing the house in flames. Floor joists and structural beams fall behind him as the fire consumes the mansion.

Ser Lucious leaves the burning structure and follows the bloodtrail to an empty stable on the estate grounds. Multiple stalls stand empty. A horse drawn coach is missing.

"I have to catch them. Emeric must be punished for his trollcraft." Lex rushes off into town, his lumbered gallop echoing through the nightfallen streets.

"He... arrives... arrives... kill him... kill... kill them.. he arrives..." the whispers return as Lex's vision blurs. Disoriented, he stumbles into the town stables, only to find that every horse including his own has been slaughtered. Beaten, slashed, and stabbed in cruel fashion. The grisly scene becomes distorted in his vision as rage overtakes him. His eyes redden, and his body twitches with involuntary spasms.

Lex turns to leave but stumbles, catching himself on the wooden doorframe. He grunts in vexation, but his voice is not his own. He tears off through the brush in shambling confusion, snarling and growling in a demonic tone as he fights to maintain control. In the near distance, he hears the howl of the ocean breeze and the crashing of water against earth. With a final mustering of strength, Lex hurls himself from the cliff and plummets towards the sea below. Midfall, as he writhes and convulses under demonic command, Lex latches the devil's shackles around his wrists. His pinioned body tumbles recklessly until it plunges into the dark ocean waters.

Lex is awakened by a loud clang. He comes into consciousness to find himself dressed in a pale grey tunic with matching drawstring pants. His balance returns, and he leaps to his bare feet to find a living nightmare. High in the air he swings within a black iron cage. Round at the top, chained to the curling, gnarled branch of a goliath oak tree.

Its form is hideous and black. From every other branch hangs a cage like his. Hundreds of them, each containing a poor soul slumped in defeat. Below him, a lifeless hellscape of jagged black rock and rivers of boiling sulfuric water emitting toxic obscuring fog. In the distance, obsidian mountains with saw toothed peaks. Looming overhead them, baleful storm clouds roil with unending lightning strikes. A disjointed orgy of screams and cries assault the senses in a sonic maelstrom.

The poisonous fog swirls and parts as a winged being flaps into view. Ebon-skinned humanoid body with long clawed limbs and a writhing ophidian tail. The creature propels itself with its crow-like wings and latches onto the branch before Lex's cage. Hanging playfully with a silken skirt swaying freely from the hips, an infernal smile cuts across its cadaverous face, as glowing blood-red eyes gleam directly into Lex's soul.

"Yaotzn'lek, where am I?" he demands, gripping his cage within white knuckled fists.

"Don't you recognize your home, slayer? This is Murkwood. The first realm of creation," the fiend laughs.

"How did you bring me here?" Lex rocks his cage with frustration.

"You are still earthbound, Ser Lex. I have full reign of your precious meat palace. And what a calamitous weapon it is," the demon sneers.

Lex growls as he begins slamming his body into the bars of the cage, attempting to break free, "NO! Release me, you vile monster!"

"You were headed here anyway. Besides, you wouldn't want to see the absolute carnage I'm sowing as we speak," Yaotzn'lek chuckles.

"You lie, devil. You're bound at the bottom of the sea," Lex snarls with his face pressed against the bars.

"Oh, yes. That silly trinket. It was quite simple to dispel. Once Cliffmoor is reduced to ash, I'm going to continue from town to town, raping and slaughtering until those pathetic humans finally kill you," the fiend rejoices.

"No. NO! I swear by all that is holy, Yaotzn'lek, that I will make you suffer! All of this will burn! MURKWOOD WILL BURN!" A boiling rage begins to consume Lex like never before.

Yaotzn'lek cocks his head back in manic laughter. "This is delicious, Ser Lex. Let it pour out. Let me taste your futile hatred. No mortal can escape these cages."

The demon's amusement shifts to concern as a blueish shimmer casts out from Lex's cage. The glow slowly shrouds every inch of Lex's powerful visage. He lifts massive hands and looks down as they burn with divine fury. He looks up to see

Yaotzn'lek frozen in fear. An emblazing blue hue shines from his vengeful gaze.

Lex charges and crashes through the bars to rip the devil from the branch, black skinned throat crunching under an iron vice grip. Black feathered wings flap about worthlessly as the two tumble hundreds of feet towards the jagged rocks below. Black blood sprays as Lex smashes his knuckles into the demon's face over and over. Yaotzn'lek gasps for air as his windpipe is slowly crushed within Lex's murderous clutch. A cloud of dust and debris tosses into the air as the demon lands back first with a thunderous slam. Engulfed in raging blue aura, Lex stands over the squirming Yaotzn'lek, broken from the treacherous plummet.

Lex hoists the fiend off his taloned feet, one wing gripped in each hand. "Your arrogance has beckoned your demise, Yaotzn'lek. I am mankind's monster. I am wrath made flesh. Heaven's righteous sword is upon your neck, pathetic demon. Now. Now, I will teach you pain!"

The fiend shrieks in anguish as Lex tears the wings from his spine. Yaotzn'lek flops face first onto the dirt with rivers of black blood pouring from the gory chasms in his back. Blood trickles on his face and tunic as Lex holds up the severed wings above his head with a triumphant roar. The suffering demon struggles to lift his battered skull.

"If I am to return to this repulsive realm they will harken my arrival with memories of terror. Nightmares of how I left your corpse."

Lex grabs the back of his bloodied skull and with one hand drags his face against the coarse volcanic rock, grating away bits of flesh. Yaotzn'lek whimpers as Lex flips him onto his back.

"Look into my eyes, Yaotzn'lek. If you are reborn, know this: if I am damned here, you will see this face as I tear the guts from your carcass over and over until time decays into oblivion."

Lex slashes the fiend's belly crossways with a shard of sharp obsidian. From the demon's throat he coughs a gurgled belch as Lex plunges his hands into his abdomen and tears forth vines of dark pink innards. Covered in gore, Lex throws down the bundle of pulsing offal and cuts loose a victorious blood-drunk warcry.

Blue energy engulfing him with even greater fervor, Lex marches to the trunk of the colossal oak. Screwed into its fleshy black bark are large iron rings anchoring the chains of the cages suspended above. One by one he rips them free with divine vigor. The cells come crashing to the ground, liberating some and killing others. The surviving freed prisoners scramble about, searching for tools and weapons. Swords, spears, chains, and makeshift clubs in the hands of freed souls as they gather around Lex.

He walks out into a barren rockscape haunted by wisps of toxic fog. With arms wide, he shouts into the bleak skies.

"Foul denizens of Murkwood! I am born of earth, here to deliver holy reckoning upon your piss-stained world! If you do not defeat us and send us back to our homes we will wage unending war against you and subjugate your whore of a queen!"

The low rumble of a horn bellows throughout the skies, quaking the ground. Thousands of black wings descend from the stormy clouds carrying armor clad legions. From the mists before them emerge horrific monstrosities of profane visage. Walking mammoths of sacrilege shake the ground with every thunderous stride. Covens of odious trolls speak obscene curses and hexes. Closing in on these meagerly equipped mortals are all the horrors of hell, leaving no possible escape.

"Brothers and sisters! Before us is a battle like never seen before. It is a fight we will not win. However, if we show what bravery burns in our hearts, then we may find salvation on the other side. If not, may word of our valor reach our kinsmen back home. So it may be known that it was not giants nor kings that marched into the belly of evil itself. It was men. Men stood against evil and never cowered! Even against the hordes of hell!"

The emblazoned Lex holds a piece of broken chain above his blood-stained face and screams, "HELL SHALL BE CONQUERED!"

Whipped into a zealous frenzy, the freed men and women charge forth in their tattered clothing, weapons in hand. Within moments the insurmountable throngs of the underworld tear into them. Stabbing, hacking, and fighting with every ounce of ferocity the mortals can muster, they respond.

But it is futile.

Demons rain spears upon them. Trolls shower them with sorcerous burning hail. Towering monstrosities snap them up into their razored jaws and devour them. Although hopeless, every last one of them fights until his last breath, rallied by the voracious words of the unlikely Lucious Lex.

The battle endures for but a few minutes. Last to fall is Ser Lucious himself, pierced through the back by a flung polearm. The wretched monsters circle around his corpse, still glowing blue. They stand in silence at a safe distance, fearful that he may rise. All around, they watch as the mortals' bodies evaporate into blue smokey essence and elevate skyward.

One by one, they vanish, returning to their fated destinations. Some to their stolen bodies, others cast into the Geistrom, the river of souls that carries one through the afterlife to be born again.

―――

Lord Emeric gazes out over the cliffside road as the red sun sinks slowly behind the ocean horizon. The cool salty breeze blows into his coach as he nurses his injured legs, tightly wrapped in gauze. He jerks forward smacking his face on one of his crutches.

"Norwyn! Norwyn you fool, why have we stopped?! Noorwyn!" Emeric freezes in horror and slowly turns his head. Standing in the coach's open door frame is a soaking wet Lucious Lex, muck and seaweed tangled throughout his armor. Before Emeric can scream, Lex lunges and grabs him by the collar. Like a mangy dog, Lex drags him from the coach and tosses him onto the ground by the cliffside.

"Norwyn! Lex is here! Kill him!" Emeric shouts.

A portly middle aged man in battered mail steps down from the driver's bench and removes his kettle helm. He stands a few heads shorter than Lex with chubby cheeks and a large bald spot on a sandy blond scalp. He stands next to the coach, bewildered.

"Lord Emeric, you were to have me thrown from the cliffs so you could laugh as I drowned. Perhaps if you were kinder to Norwyn, he may have tried. But now, I'm going to have you tossed from the cliffs... for your despicable practices."

Lex turns to Norwyn and nods. The pudgy guard walks over to the battered lord Emeric as he cries and pleads. Norwyn grips him by the collar and waistband as he flails about. With a heave-ho, the guard hucks the petulant nobleman over the cliff. A waning scream tapers off as he plummets onto the rocks below. A few white waves wash his broken corpse out with the tide.

"His gold is in a locker in the back trunk. Take it, Ser Lex. I won't fight you," Norwyn says as he stares down at his boots.

Lex smashes the lock and rips the trunk open to reveal a large chest overflowing with gems and gold coin. "I don't see his gold. I only see your gold, Lord Norwyn. I just need to borrow a pursefull. Enough for some ale, a whore, and a hot bath. I'm taking one of your horses as well. You owe me a horse."

Norwyn looks around dumbfounded as Ser Lucious Lex unbridles one of the black stallions and mounts it.

"Forgive me for my rushed leave. It's been a long day. I feel like I've been to hell and back."

Norwyn scratches his bald head as Ser Lucious Lex gallops off down the road.

She Has Arrived
From The Bizarchives Issue #4

"For over six hundred years I have served the council! I was on the frontlines of the mongrel incursion! Do you know how much I've sacrificed for this dome?!" Karl Beorn shouts at the lean doctor.

"I understand your frustration, my good Karl. However, I cannot in good faith administer another rejuvenation treatment. Your record shows that you've already had twelve. Studies prove that many patients begin to show signs of delirium after only five," the doctor explains calmly.

"You wouldn't even be standing here if it wasn't for my service to this dome!" the Karl exclaims in outrage, throwing up his hands and flopping backwards onto the examination table. He pushes his forehead into his palms in crushing disappointment. The doctor puts his touchscreen down and rolls his stool up to the sighing Karl and comforts him with a pat on the shoulder. "My dear Karl, you've lived a wonderfully long life, decorated with an endless list of achievements. You could very easily live another forty or even sixty years," the doctor reassures him.

"With my luck, I will live another two centuries and have

another thirty six wives until I die in disgrace without a single child to my name," Karl Beorn laments.

"My dear Karl, you are one of the most celebrated men in Adland Dome. These feelings of disgrace are all in your head," the doctor says in an attempt to reassure him. Karl Beorn nods in silence and stands up from the table before exiting through the quasi-translucent automatic door.

Karl Beorn takes an unscheduled detour through the city streets of the highborn business quarter. He can't remember the last time he took an unscheduled stroll through the city. In fact, he can't remember the last time he did anything unscheduled. His centuries of life have been spent with his nose to the grindstone. Everything was planned, focused and according to schedule without a second thought to his surroundings.

But this route has the scent of *déjà vu*. The dark, metal highrises and spired buttresses feel eerily familiar. The Karl feels a comforting solitude, not being surrounded by an entourage of guards and advisors like in his political days as Drighten advisory board member. It feels good to be just a face in the crowd.

The city is quite beautiful. The typical auburn twilight of the black dragon sun is washed out by the jubilant blinking and flashing of the neon tracks ascending up the corners of the stoic housing structures.

"Ah yes, Teela and I walked down this street during our courtship."

Beorn smiles. His smile slowly fades into a look of sorrow. He realizes that he has been so busy that he has forgotten about his beloved first wife.

A gentle graze of cool wind brushes against his face. In his deep pontification, the Karl loses track of his location. He crosses the business quarter and leaves across a quaint little pedestrian bridge. Beorn stops and peers down at the waist-high metal wall. "Skolwern" is carved into it. "Great divine. It's still here," Beorn reminisces. For the first time in centuries he can recall Teela's face.

"My sweet Teela. This is where you first let me kiss you. I can't believe that after all of these years it is still here. My heart never healed after the plague took you from me. Those dozens of other relationships were set to fail: none of them were you. At your passing, I promised that I would never forget you. I broke that promise. I forgot you." A single tear trickles down the Karl's stoic face.

"I wonder if Kade's Hall is still around, I could use some stiff wine. If the lowborn do one thing right, it's drinking away their problems." Beorn runs his fingers across the graffiti one last time and continues his trek.

The city hasn't changed in a millennium. Dark steel buildings jammed together like the crowded teeth of a mongrel's mouth. Buildings are built on buildings, resembling more a fungal colony than a dwelling for humans. A haunting mash of gothic architecture with neon tracks and floating projected billboards display advertisements for the cracker plant and a myriad of back-alley watering holes. The further one ventures from the bustling business and residential districts of the highborn, the more one's vision is obscured by the lingering smog expelled by the numerous industrial smoke stacks that line the distant undercity.

It is an unequaled privilege to be highborn, for those who live above the partition enjoy synthetic UV nourishment and air filtration. However, the overwhelming majority of Adland Dome's citizens live below the highrises and buttresses, never seeing the horizon of obsidian spires nor the backdrop of the red glow blurred by the dome's ionized liquidity. Most have never left their slums and the endless miles of featureless corridors to even see the dome. Most lowborn probably don't even know it exists nor would they care. Regardless, all of Adland are imprisoned in the grim twilight of the dome. It is a dystopian cell but also their only salvation.

The Karl's keen ears hear the clapping of boots smacking across the puddled pavement approaching from behind. With lightning reflexes, Beorn spins around, naturally placing his right foot back in a defensive stance. Before him stand two filthy-faced lowborn men in tattered grey jumpsuits both brandishing shanks. The Karl could identify their lowborn status instantly as they both stood at least two heads shorter than the aging Karl. Even at his hyper advanced age he was still of superior physique and stature due his highborn pedigree.

"I will transfer one hundred Skales into each of your accounts if you place your blades onto the ground and return to your homes," Karl Beorn offers in a stern tone.

"Heh, or we could stick you like a pigrat and take everything. Whadda you gonna do to stop us?" one of the undercity laborers scoffs.

"One hundred Skales is double a week's salary at the cracker plant. Please, young man, I'm sure you have families. That's why you're attempting this. Just take the-"

Before the Karl could finish negotiating, the lowborn rush him. One charges straight for his torso with his blade outstretched, the other leaps through the air, both hands on the makeshift pommel, attempting to plunge it downward into Beorn's throat.

With unnatural quickness, the Karl sidesteps the initial charge, redirecting the lowborn's momentum and grabbing him from behind. A look of horror freezes on the leaping man's face as he accidentally plunges his blade into his comrade's throat which the Karl has placed in his knife's trajectory. The man gargles as blood sprays out of his esophagus, spattering his friend's face and blinding him. With a swift forward kick to the chest, the Karl send the blood-painted lowborn tumbling backwards; his knife goes skipping across the concrete. He watches on in horror as the Karl grapples his opponent's blade away from him and gruesomely slashes the man's open throat across his entire neck. Beorn grips his chin upward, and blood quickly drains from his neck before he tosses his twitching corpse to the ground.

The Karl holds up his bloody hands, revealing his palms in a gesture of truce as the now disarmed lowborn climbs to his feet shaking in rage and grief.

"Bekert, he's dead. You fucking bastard!" The man howls in hate as he charges again, this time fists clenched. With a blinding snapkick, Beorn splits his attacker's knee backwards. His leg broken and limp, the would-be avenger falls forward into a guillotine headlock. With a chilling crack, the lowborn's head is twisted and arches backwards. His pale, lifeless body collapses, his unsupported head unnaturally flopping to the side. Karl Beorn gazes down at the ghastly faces of his murdered victims, permanently seized into twisted expressions of pain with mouths agape. For the first time in years, his stoic expression is broken by a pursed frown as his eyes swell with uncontrollable tears.

"I..I'm a monster.." the Karl sobs, placing his palm over his quivering lips. "Two families torn apart. Children orphaned so that one barren old fool can continue drawing breath for four more loathsome decades," he whispers into his hands as he clutches his tear stained face.

Beorn slowly turns and continues into the bowels of the partition slums with a slouched lumber. As he traipses down back alleys and populated pedestrian streets, the many undercity denizens stop their business to stare at the tear soaked nobleman, his pale blue jumper still spattered with fresh blood. For hours the Karl wanders in a mournful daze, rambling under his breath. Upon seeing the filthy highborn in his estranged state, lowborn mothers quickly shuttle their children into their makeshift hovels.

The Adland slums resemble a dark steel anthive with perpendicular hallways fashioned into living quarters, cordoned off with scrap metal sliding doors. Many levels beneath the surface, the lowborn unfortunate enough to call this place home live in abject squalor. At one time these structures were factory corridors but they were abandoned centuries ago. The further down you go, the lower the ceilings and the shorter its inhabitants become. Along each main hallway ceiling are poorly powered lighting tracks that illuminate the space with a never ending orange glow.

There is no day or night here, only the dim orange light.

On occasion, the old batteries that keep these forgotten dwellings going will expire, trapping those inside in an unnavigable darkness. A few will escape to neighboring slum blocks, but most will perish. If communication or travel from a nearby slum ceases, the lowborn there will assume they *went black*. A grim reality that all lowborn this far beyond the partition always have in the back of their minds: that they are living on borrowed time. It could be tomorrow or in another century but inevitably every slum will eventually *go black*.

"Sweet divine, what happened to you?" A soft feminine voice interrupts Beorn's daze. His erratic lurch comes to a halt. The usually immaculately groomed Karl now filthy and disheveled, turns and looks with dark-bagged eyes reddened from the flow of tears. He peers down to see a small portly middle-aged woman with swarthy features and big caring eyes. Despite her dress being fashioned from recovered cracker plant uniforms, it was nicely tailored.

"I am lost," the towering Karl mutters.

"Lost in many ways it looks like," the woman replies as she gently rubs Beorn's forearm. "You're not safe out here. How

She Has Arrived

about joining me and my daughter for dinner? You can rest and get your wits about you." The woman reassures him.

"Bringing a stranger into your home? Are you not worried that I could be dangerous?" Beorn asks.

With a pursed smirk, the woman tugs his arm and leads him forward. "Yes, I'm sure a noble born councilman is going to rob me of my scrap kitchen utensils." She chuckles. "Besides, I'm sure council administration will reward me for helping you. Now hurry, before dinner burns."

The woman leads him into her abode.

The shanty dwelling is bleak but has a homely quality. Hanging from the dark steel walls are neatly pressed cloths cleverly dyed with vibrant designs like decorative tapestries. A soldered basin and gas burner compose a makeshift kitchen at the far end of the single room dwelling. Above them swing several pieces of scrap bent and shaped into various kitchen utensils. On either side, chained to the walls, hang fold out cots fashioned from plastic wall paneling. The bedding is sewn together from discarded plant worker uniforms.

"Please sit, my daughter will be home any second with water, then we can eat." The woman gestures to a knee-high blacksteel slab propped up by plastex block. Around it sit a few handmade floor cushions. After a few moments, the door cloth splits and a youthful figure enters the room carrying a sloshing canister. The Karl stares in awe at the homely girl as she lugs the water right by him and into the kitchen area. Her long tufted brown hair is bundled up with cord, holding it from falling in front of her soft angular face. Her dress is fashioned like her mother's but with small decorative variations.

"Sir Karl, this is my daughter Jaqtira," the mother says, introducing the girl as she places a steaming pot on the table next to a stack of tin bowls.

Her daughter casts a friendly smile and waves daintily. "Call me Jackie".

Jackie's low bred lineage is clearly presented in her meager stature, bad posture and swarthy complexion. Deep set expressionless dark eyes on a long filthy face. Certainly prettier than most of her under city kinsmen but still bearing their cursed features. She pours herself a bowl of the steaming soup and begins to eat, seemingly unaware of the Karl's unbreaking, hungering stare. Between spoonfuls she occasionally peers up to meet his obsessive gaze with an innocent smile completely oblivious of his intention. After several minutes, she finishes her bowl and thanks her mother for dinner before scurrying off. Every move is intensely observed by an unmoving Beorn.

Karl Beorn turns to her mother who had watched the entire exchange in evident discomfort, a worried look upon her rosy face.

"I love your daughter," he says with labored breath as he longingly stares at the doorway.

"Eat your dinner and lay down for a while. It seems you aren't feeling well," the mother suggests.

She is startled as he pounds his fists against the table in frustration "No! I'm fine! I saw my physician this morning and he said that I could live for another sixty years!"

To any underborn this statement would have been confusing as they rarely even live to be that old. The unfortunate lifespan of those beyond the partition awards them an average of just forty-five years. The rejuvenation treatments commonly used by the highborn are not only inaccessible to lower castes, they would probably disregard them as tall tales if presented with the concept.

The Karl softens his tone and continues, "I am one of the wealthiest men in the dome. Whatever price you can dream of, I will double it. Triple it. I will transfer it right now so you and all

She Has Arrived

of your loved ones will never have to toil again. Your children and your children's children will never know hunger again. You can all leave all of this behind forever, I promise."

Tears begin to swell in his eyes "I love Jackie. Please... I beg of you. Allow her to be my wife." He takes the mother's hand and kneels before her.

After a few silent moments of flustered pontification, the mother nods her head in agreement. She then turns and pokes her head out of the entrance to summon her daughter. Jaqtira comes wandering in with a look of confusion.

"Yes, Mama?"

"Jaqtira, sweetheart. After your father and brother never came home we've really struggled. I always said that a good man would come into your life and lift us all out of the hard times," her mama explains, petting her hair.

"Well, Jaqtira, he's here. Sir Beorn is a Karl. They live in big tall dwellings on the surface. They eat meat every night and sleep in big soft cots. Their water is clean and they take medicine to cure sickness. Their homes have many rooms where they play games and listen to music. You're going to live with them. You're going to be Karl Beorn's wife." She chokes

"But Mama, I can't leave you behind." Jackie pouts.

"Karl Beorn has given us a very, very big gift. I can use it to buy a home on the partition. I'm going to bring Milas, Carra and Tum with me, along with their families. We won't be far. No more pigrat soup for us. Jaqtira, great divine has blessed us." She hugs her daughter before leading her to Karl Beorn who stands hunched under the low ceiling. He embraces her in his powerful arms and they exit together.

The dim red glow of the irradiated sky leaks down through the smoggy air of the dome. Lead by the hand, Jaqtira emerges from the dark corridor in awe. Frozen, she looks out into the expanse of the dome megalopolis for the first time. Slowly, she walks over to the catwalk rail for a better look. Endless spirescapes spread out below and above her with millions of nameless souls scurrying and toiling on walkways and ledges. She gasps as a floating neon advertisement drifts overhead. The humming roar of its hover engines sends vibrations down her spine. Beorn pulls back his sleeve, still stained with blood, to reveal a touch screen bracelet. Jackie looks on bewildered at its pale blue illumination.

"Welcome to the world, my love. Don't be frightened, I'll teach you everything," Beorn tenderly reassures her. He draws a long retractable cord from his bracelet and plugs it into a nearby terminal. After a few presses and toggles, he pulls the plug free and allows it to recoil and snap back into place. Soon afterwards, a craft approaches. The chrome-paneled, pill-shaped vessel slowly docks next to the catwalk. Vertically hinged doors split and open to reveal a lavish red velour interior. Steps with decorative gold rails fold out before them. Beorn aids Jackie up the stairs and into a luxury taxi that looks more akin to a presidential suite than a passenger vessel. She covers her ears and looks frantically about trying to figure out the source of an archaic piano ballad.

"Music off, please," Beorn commands.

"Right away, sir. And to where are you headed, Sir Karl?" a voice replies over the speaker.

"Drighton's Gardens, please, first quarter," he answers.

Jackie clutches the gold-trimmed upholstery in fear as the coach takes off. Beorn holds her tightly to calm her. The short flight comes to an end as the unseen pilot completes a brief landing protocol. Hydraulic hisses fill the air, and the doors open again.

Jackie's eyes widen with confusion and awe as they step out into the highborn residential district. Rows of opulent manors fill the space, shared with sprawling lush gardens. Vines and ivy dangle over pearlish stone walkways. Flowers of purple, red and blue bloom in all directions, covering the walls and the pristine marble fountains. Every mansion doorway is wide and high with decorative arches. As they walk hand in hand, the highborn passersby stare in confusion. Jaqtira returns their looks in kind. The contrast between the two castes could not be more dramatic. She was like a goblin amongst gods.But Beorn doesn't care as he leads her to his manor. Her shock only grows as she enters his luxuriant estate.

Weeks pass, but Jackie from below the partition never acclimates to her new environment. Overstimulated and confused, she sinks more and more into herself, speaking less and less. However, Karl Beorn's obsessive behavior only intensifies. He dresses her in the finest robes and hires the best beauticians. Every night he rolls out a sumptuous dinner that she barely touches. Like a decorative china doll, she sits at his side staring blankly. Every day he pampers her and every night she lies still as he seeds her.

One night, a peculiar man carrying an insulated briefcase arrives. The case contains vials of a glowing green liquid.

"These are the fertility treatments you've ordered, sir Karl. Cutting edge. It's a gene therapy not dissimilar to the rejuvenation treatments you've had," the hook-nosed, half-caste boasts.

"And you assure me that they are safe? They won't harm my wife?" Beorn asks as Jaqtira looks at the vials with a cold, detached expression.

"They are immensely safe. Cutting edge. They will be available to the public as soon as the council stops dragging their feet with their bureaucratic nonsense. You were in council. You know better than I do how slow and tedious their decisions can be," the man says as he adjusts his collar.

"I can't believe it. This is our dream come true! My love, we will finally be with child. I will be a father. My curse is lifted!" Beorn showers Jaqtira with kisses; she awkwardly reciprocates but says nothing.

The doctor pulls out a syringe and draws the viridescent ooze. One vial after another, Jackie is injected with the concoction. As soon as the doctor leaves, Beorn leads her to the bedroom. For the time being, this is where most of their time is spent. Day after day of desperate insemination becomes weeks until she finally becomes pregnant.

Jubilant and maddened, Karl Beorn is completely unaware of the irregularities of her gestation. Extreme sickness and pain befall her. The fetus in her womb grows to full size too rapidly. The normal bumps and flutters of a healthy child *in utero* are violent and unnatural. In just eleven weeks, Jaqtira's waters break and Karl Beorn rushes her to the infirmary in the highborn business quarter.

Jackie shrieks in excruciating pain as her body contracts and bloats. Her stomach is pressed upon from within by wild thrashing shapes. The doctors and nurses gag and recoil at the stench emitted by the yellowish slop oozing from her womb. Beorn cheers it on with celebratory tears in his eyes, unphased by the grotesque display before him. With a bloodcurdling scream, she howls and pushes. From her body comes a wet crunching sound as what infests her insides is vomited into a cold steel tray. The doctors look on in horror at the mockery of nature before them.

In a swamp of curdled puss and steaming blood-streaked yellow discharge lies a squirming grotesquery. Short boneless legs fused together like an ophidian appendage. Its torso hairless and shriveled with a ribless chest revealing its pulsating insides with each groaning breath. An oblong eyeless skull, crowded with hooked fangs emerging from bloodied black gums.

"She's.... she's beautiful..." Beorn lifts the writhing creature from the pan, his eyes streaming with tears of happiness. His lips meet the child's soft skull for a kiss. Strings of yellow slime peel away and dangle from his mouth. The hideous infant gurgles and growls as it flounders in his loving embrace.

"Jaqtira, my queen. Look at our baby girl. Look at our angel. I'm going to name her *Teela*." Beorn approaches Jackie, bloodied and exhausted on the hospital cot.

As Beorn comes closer, Jackie recoils and her labored breaths become frantic sobs.

"Take it away, please. Please get it away from me," she whimpers between her cries.

"Don't fret my love. The pain is over. She has arrived. Our princess has arrived," Beorn continues speaking as he moves closer.

"No! Stay away from me! I wish I had never came here. I hate you. I HATE YOU! You're a MONSTER!" Her head jerks backwards as a chunk of her skull is vaporized by the blaster in Beorn's hand.

The doctor leaps to the wall and presses buttons to sound the alarm. A rapid succession of precise blaster shots kills every nurse in the delivery room, one by one..

"Karl, Karl Beorn. Please re-...relax," the doctor pleads, holding his shaking hands up in fear. "You know blasters are outlawed within the dome."

"Thank you for your help, doctor." Two blaster shots caulderize holes through the doctor's chest as he collapses lifeless to the floor.

With the monstrous child secured in his arms, the delirious

Karl walks out onto the street, covered in blood and putrid afterbirth. The highborn denizens flee in terror as Beorn mercilessly guns them down, leaving carnage in his wake. Alarms sound throughout the streets, cutting through the frantic chorus of screams and cries. The trigger clicks empty, and Beorn discards the spent weapon. With a flick of his arm a blade telescopes from a hilt, deftly drawn from his belt. Centuries of combat training and the expeience of hundreds of battles prove the Karl to be an adept butcher of men. Even among his highborn peers he moves with superior reflex, slashing flesh from bodies like birthday cake.

The clacking of dozens of boots echos through the streets as the dome police force closes in. Beorn ceases his slaughter and flees leaping over dividers and walls with ease. Hopping from platform to platform he escapes his pursuers. He sprints through the business quarters and stops to catch his breath on a pedestrian bridge crossing from the highborn sectors, leading down into the partition. He stops for a brief moment and looks down at the disfigured creature in his arms. In the distance he hears the hover engines and the sirens of approaching police craft.

"No..no no. Don't worry Teela. Daddy's here. Daddy will never let them hurt you. Daddy loves you, my sweet sweet baby girl. I promise that daddy will never let them hurt you." He wipes his tears away with his blood-drenched sleeve.

"Daddy's gonna take you to see mommy. You're going to go see mommy in heaven. There, she will see how beautiful you are. She'll see what I see. My sweet, sweet angel," he whispers, rocking the baby.

Beorn walks up and runs his fingers across some graffiti carved into the bridge wall that reads "Skolwern". He steps onto the wall of the bridge as a police craft shines a spotlight on him from the air.

"You're going to go see mommy now. They won't be able to hurt you there. Daddy isn't coming. Because monsters don't go to heaven."

Clutching the baby in both arms, Karl Beorn falls forward. Both plummet headfirst hundreds of feet before splattering onto the dark steel platform below. Scatterings of unrecognizable meat are strewn across the platform. Sirens and cries echo in the distance as a crowd forms around the remnants of Karl Beorn and his beloved daughter.

A council meeting is called, overseen by the Drighton himself. He rules that Karl Beorn's centuries of service and bravery are not to be erased because of delirium. Despite the loss of life and the mayhem, his death should be viewed as a tragedy of mental breakdown. As a result, rejuvenation treatments are limited by law to only one. All of Beorn's estate is awarded to his first wife Atia, including his cat Teela.

Nothing is ever transferred to Jaqtira's mother. A day after the tragedy, her entire slumblock mysteriously went black. None of her community escaped.

They Never Woke Up
From The Bizarchives Issue $1

"He's alive."

"Can you hear me, friend?"

The creaky rattle of the cheap metal cot disturbed Gert's corpse-like slumber. "Wake up my friend, we are the only ones left," the man's gently pitched voice repeated as Gert struggled to lift his eyelids.

"W-what happened?" Gert responded before turning his head to finally get a look at the phantom voice pulling him into consciousness.

"We're the only ones who survived the night. Dome life support must've failed in the night as a radiation storm passed through. An unfortunate coincidence but not uncommon. It happened to one of my previous digs about eighty years ago."

"Eighty years ago?" Gert puzzled.

"Yes, I am three hundred and twenty-six years old. I've had only four rejuvenation treatments too!" the man boasted.

Gert lurched up, still slightly disoriented, peering upon the man from his waist-high bed perch, a bed that resembled more of an operating table than a cot and with similar discomfort as well. The articulate fellow spoke with the haught only a highborn caste would carry but was pleasant enough. He looked to be of middle age, with poker-straight black hair slicked sideways with a shaven undercut on the opposite side. A popular hairstyle among socialites above the partition. Despite his age, the aristocrat kept an impressive physique displayed by tightly fit coverall, one piece of pale blue with white track stripe down the sides. His black utility belt was outfitted with several instruments and gadgets unidentifiable to Gert.

Gert finally stood up noticing that his new acquaintance dwarfed him standing around 6'4". The well-bred highborn were always of impressive stature. A relieved smile widened on the highborn's long, handsome face as he extended his hand for a shake. "Karl Svei Brennik, it's a pleasure."

"Gert," he replied as Karl Brennik enveloped his hand and proceeded to shake with confidence.

"A lowborn out here at a dig? Are you exalted?" the Karl asked.

"I am," replied Gert. "I was awarded this mission due to my exceptional service in the cracker plant. Ten years without a single absence. So, the partition clerk recommended me for advanced labor. I accepted without a second thought," Gert explained.

"That is certainly quite the achievement, my friend. It's always refreshing to hear stories like yours. Many above the partition simply believe the lowborn are all petty criminals or even a smidge above mongrelmen," scoffed Brennik.

Gert grit his teeth at the thought of ungrateful highborn limpwrists but restrained from the usual resentful tirade as it is unwise to insult a highborn to their face, especially one as sympathetic as the Karl. "I've always wondered, what's the 'Karl' stuff all about anyway?" Gert asked bluntly.

"Well, Gert, a Karl is a highborn bearing blood relation to the Drighten himself. It is a title of nobility within the hierarchy of Adland Dome," the Karl explained. "We are, from birth, groomed and educated to be High Councilmen," he continued. "Most stick to their studies, their athletics and their politics, never leaving the dome. I suffer from wanderlust and have found myself specializing in the study of the forgotten world. I may be a black sheep back in the court but none have the spine to tell me to my face. So, as your fellow lowborn would say, *fuck 'em*."

Gert snorted a chuckle at the unexpected vulgarity of the Karl, as it was widely considered unbecoming of a noble to curse like undertown riff-raff. Both of the men erupted in laughter, seemingly unaware of their grim surroundings. In this long, one-room temporary structure were lines of metal cots identical to Gert's. Each pushed against the plastic paneled wall, each with a round locker at the bedfoot and each inhabited by a lifeless laborer laying still in their unexpected deathbeds. Each corpse purple in the face from being poisoned by irradiated air. No life support system to protect them.

Their faces twisted into unnatural expressions of unspeakable anguish. Streaks of dried blood trickled from tear ducts housing bulging bright red eyes protruding from their orbital sockets, as if they had been squeezed out like some gruesome carnival toy.

"Every building is the same scene. Poor bastards," Karl Brennik sympathized as the dim blink of the near terminal illuminated his sorrowful face. "Let's go outside and wait. I've reactivated the power core. As soon as the system reboots we'll be able to radio for transport. When we get back I'll be sure to wire a few extra skales to the families of these poor men. I can't imagine how heartbroken their wives will be."

The men exited the building into the red twilight of the dome. No city, settlement, colony or encampment can survive these lands for long periods without life-dome technology. A veil of energy emitted from several nodes in a circular formation will encapsulate anything within, protecting the inhabitants from radiation, dust storms, solar flares, and blast weapons. They even repelled marauding beasts with a low frequency sound that was painful to their ears.

Their boots crunched the gravely texture of the reddish brown topsoil, avoiding patches of sparse grass and vegetation. Even though it was unlikely within the dome to be attacked, small patches of grass could conceal various toxic critters that would lunge out and bite any unwary passerby. One such creature was the gorecrab, a grotesque little insect that scurried up untucked pant legs and sunk its sharp claws into a poor victim's skin so they may inject their flesh eating larvae. Someone bitten by the gorecrab would have roughly two hours before the worms burrowed their way to the brain, where they formed cocoons until it became time to hatch and emerge from the host's skull, which would split like a rotten pumpkin.

"Karl Brennik? Let's say the radio doesn't work. How far of a trek is it back to Adland Dome?" Gert asked.

"Let's hope the radio works. It's a hel of a walk across the Redlands, through the Soulrot Canyon and then north over Whore's Hills to Adland Dome. We survived one mishap, I'd prefer not to attempt two. And that's if ASCENSION doesn't intercept our radio transmission and triangulate our location."

"What's ASCENSION? Some kind of mongrel cult?" Gert inquired.

"ASCENSION is an artificial intelligence core. Nobody knows where they reside, how they live. All we know is this AI unit breeds humans to serve the machine. That's the reason we use all closed circuit systems for communication. ASCENSION will infiltrate, infect and exterminate all inhabitants," Brennik warned.

"How have I never heard this?!" Gert spat.

"This is common knowledge among the Council. It's an existential threat and we're constantly working to protect Adland. If the lowborn were told of this, there would be panic and paranoia. They do not know. Let's keep it that way. You're a fine fellow, Mister Gert, but it's well within my power to send word and have you erased. Please don't make me exercise that."

Gert nodded silently. "You said they? There's a lot of them? What do they look like?" he continued questioning with a rattled tone.

"Yes, there's a lot of them. With unknown genetic science they breed these men in synthetic bags. Artificial wombs. Well, I'm not sure they can be called *men*. They are neither man nor woman. The machine edited out reproductive organs. They're called *asapiens*. That's all we know. We don't even know what they eat or how they live. They obliterate entire colonies and reap their resources. That's why digs like these are so important. We've found evidence that the people of the forgotten world were all fertile. Couples could birth two or even three offspring per family in a lowborn lifespan." Karl Brennik's dissertation was interrupted by the accelerating hum of the system reboot.

"Ah! We are saved. I'll go unlock the radio terminal. We'll be out of this cemetery in no time." Karl Brennik hopped up from sitting on his travel pack and began walking in the direction of a westward building. He approached a broad box-shaped terminal. Around the light blue projected touch screen was a myriad of tangled wires, all weaving to unknown inputs, and the top was decorated with a series of peculiarly shaped antennas jettisoning out the top like an archaic crown. The Karl reached down to begin typing a varied sequence, but the screen was obscured by a splatter of blood. Wide-eyed, Brennik screamed, but only a grotesque gurgle of blood began to pour from his mouth as Gert yanked the boot knife from the side of his throat.

Brennik collapsed forward on top of the terminal. He tried to claw at the machine in a feeble attempt to escape as Gert frantically plunged his blade into his back over and over. The bloodied highborn convulsed uncontrollably as rivers of dark blood gushed out of every new wound in his body. Sliding from the blood soaked terminal box, the Karl fell backward to flip flat on his back. Less a precise assassin and more like a sweatshop butcher, Gert continued his assault, stabbing and ripping like a deranged animal with cold, emotionless eyes.

Gert stood up, towering over the twitching body as the final shallow breaths of life fled from the highborn's mutilated lungs. Gert leaned down and jiggled the freshly dead Karl's jaw to ensure the murder was complete. It was. The mangled corpse was as still as those in the cots as the ocean of blood around him slowly poured out like a horrific halo. Gert drew a strange syringe from his belt pouch, and from its cylinder a long syringe telescoped out. He slowly plunged the needle into the dead aristocrat's chest and withdrew the pink-red internal fluid. Stepping over the butchered mess of a man, Gert calmly walked over to the communications terminal and entered a sequence of codes. The bloody terminal emitted the scratch of radio frequency. "A1G73, the colony has been exterminated, genetics have been extracted; was my correspondence with the ape recorded?" Gert spoke coldly into the terminal.

A scrambled reply came. "Correspondence documented. Retrieval entering dome now".

The energy field slowly dissipated as a small squad of hairless, androgynous humanoids approached. All of them fitted with off-white jumpers and bearing tall backpacks adorned with various bizarre instruments. "Gert" stood upright and motionless like a mannequin as the squad approached. At his feet they placed a knee-high rectangular box, as deep as it was tall. A small panel of buttons with a sliding hatch door was on its lid. Upon meeting, no greetings or etiquettes were shared. Only cold stares. The squad leader held out his hand. "Gert" placed the syringe vial into his palm and it was quickly put inside a pouch on the squad leader's belt.

"You have fulfilled your purpose of creation, A1G73. It is time to be cycled." The leader spoke plainly.

Gert nodded, and crouched down to the ground to lay on his back. The squad encircled him, drawing strange surgical circular saws. While completely conscious, the asapiens began to dismember Gert with surgical precision like some soulless, grotesque ritual. All dismembered body parts were placed in the top of the strange box device, until finally Gert's head was all that was left. It was placed in an unfolded black bag, which emitted gaseous cool air upon opening. The head was swiftly tucked into a squad backpack and lifted off.

The squad leader pressed a series of buttons on the box device. It began to vibrate as the inner toothed cogs ground and mulched the fleshly contents. It churned and shook as the ghoulish machine resonated the muffled sounds of tearing and grinding what was the facsimile of a man only minutes ago. The machine let out a chilling steam as it vomited out a perfectly formed bar the size of a phonebook in its rear chute.

The squad leader picked it up and handed it to a comrade. "Place this in sustenance revisions. It will be required as we revitalize this colony. Call for brooding pods. We will need to continue the dig and retrieve all knowledge for hive mother. This world will soon be cured of humanity."

Human Candles

Some years ago, during my brief stint haunting the halls of the University of Pennsylvania, I met a man of untold genius. An exceptional mind that rose far beyond the hinderances of the institutional intelligentsia. It was 1898, the Spanish-American war was at full thrust and I, an aspiring academic, was pining for a career in the natural sciences. However, despite my best efforts, my marks were lacking prestige.

Hailing from a familial background of studious and learned men, I greatly desired to carry the torch. Folding my hand at university and settling for a livelihood among the laboring class would've been interpreted by my family as a stain upon their reputation as proper Yankee aristocrats. A prejudice I found haughty, but nonetheless, if I wanted my right to inheritance, one must acquiesce on such infinitesimal traditions.

It was a particularly stormy summer in Philadelphia of 1898. Many evenings, I scampered urgently down the flooded cobbled streets, clinging dearly to my bowler as the howling wind tried to tear it from my thinning crown. The hardwood hallways at the university residence hall on such occasions looked more akin to a trawler deck than a dormitorium. Despite its dampness, the hall was a place of stimulation and camaraderie. Students, tutors and traveling professors found interest among the many debates and discussions often had over foaming pewter steins. The halls and harrows echoing with the murmuring song of intellectual chatter or the occasional rowdy banter.

It was one evening in particular when I met the eccentric Dr. Piers William Levick. A man some twenty years my senior with thick swarthy features and ovular spectacles. He was of slight build and spoke with a noticeable frontal lisp. The students would oft rib about his manner of speech with an impression of "*Dr. Peerth, at your thervith*". A man of easy demeanor, Dr. Levick would indulge their hecklings by responding with one of his many avoided words. My favorite of his butchered pronunciations being "presumptuous",

Upon our first meeting at one of the many uniformly arranged mess tables, Dr. Levick unfurled a lengthy dissertation outlining his idealist weltanschauung. And with every refill of lager, he unraveled an ever more unorthodox theorem. You see, Dr. Piers Levick was a premier of the progressivist ideology, albeit an unusual variety. While his contemporaries championed revolutionary enlightenment philosophies, he argued that such positions were milquetoast, and that focus should be upon a strive towards scientific apotheosis. Despite being an esteemed expert in biology and natural sciences, Dr. Levick considered the academies as rigid materialists doomed to mundane and inconsequential discoveries due to their narrow understanding of truth.

Having a young man's streak of innate rebellious spirit, I found his dissident critique of the institutions to be wildly intriguing. I found myself attending all of his lectures and burying my nose in any literature of his recommendation. I became Dr. Levick's most ardent pupil. And as I ventured further into his tutelage, the more adept I became. My other coursework that felt daunting months prior, quickly became rudimentary for me.

One morning after Levick concluded a particular instruction, I noticed an odd tome of antiquity among his notes. A worn leather-bound book with symbolic engravings on the cover. This artefact struck my curiosity. After some reluctance, he explained that it was the records of experimentation from one, John Dee. A 16th century occultist and mathematician who claimed to have communed with angelic entities through scrying. The act of meditational focus into a reflective surface in order to contact metaphysical or supradimensional beings. I was unsure of the validity of such practice, but my mentor appeared quite enthralled by what he called "alchemy". An antiquated conception of science that the most credentialed sort would consider below their acumen.

It was then, Dr. Levick proposed I become his aid in his private research efforts and help man his laboratory. With a stoic face he warned that none of our research may be seen by anyone else for any reason. That this was his life work to be guarded in secrecy at all costs and any breach would be repaid with the absolute most severe of consequences. Without hesitation I accepted and signed a contract he presented.

The subsequent weeks were devoted to attempting to

measure and document the environment during a successful scrying session. This proved problematic as almost all self-proclaimed occultists who participated in the study failed to demonstrate any sort of ability. After dozens of failed attempts, a subject of peculiar visage arrived to participate. She was unusually tall for a woman and hid her face behind an oriental silk scarf. The control room was a small area of common design. In the middle, sat an angled wooden desk with the black scrying mirror before it. In the back sat Dr. Levick and I.

The woman entered with little interaction and sat at the desk. After an hour or so of indecipherable whispered chants, she appeared to enter a focused state. As she rocked to and fro, her eyes winced visibly, and she began to perspire. Our lab tables were outfitted with various peculiar and archaic instruments. Metal orbs dangling from wires, swaying antennae and copper tuning forks. As her focus began to crescendo, to our shock and surprise, the forks hummed with vibrational energy. In unison with the forks, a swirling and disjointed apparition appeared in the mirror's glass. Then in a moment it all abruptly stopped.

With a deep breath the occultist woman calmly rose to her feet and approached us. Staring straight at the door, she spoke in a hoarse voice.

"You will find what you seek, boys. Unfortunately." She said as she turned the bronze door handle before passing into the dark hallway.

Dr. Levick and I were at a loss for words. Staring at one another with widened eyes of profundity. After numerous fruitless experiments, this one mysterious woman provided exactly the results we so desperately desired. Immediately, Dr. Levick began speculating upon what may have been the source of causation, what she and the magicians of old could have channeled in order to emit this energy.

I raised concerns about the cryptic warning she proposed before taking her leave. That our experimentation would yield an unfortunate outcome. However, such concerns were wholly ignored as if Dr. Levick heard nothing of the sort. He was drunk with intrigue, and nothing could break his focus.

After much pontification, Dr. Levick lifted his finger in an epiphany. "Pain! Focused pain!" He shouted.

"If you noticed, my good lad. Our subject seemed to have been forcing herself into a meditative state of suffering. It's widely known that such states emit signals, vibrations perhaps when one experiences extreme pain. Many studies demonstrate that twins will experience shared pain or be alerted to the condition of their sibling even though they are not present," Levick said.

This revelation led to a peculiar series of experimentation. Under Dr. Levick's order I went about the city to find downtrodden and derelict individuals willing to participate for small amounts of compensation. Individuals who, due to their desperate circumstances, have less regard for their personal well-being, hobos, urchins and the like. Despite their reprobate nature, many of these sorts were restive in regard to agreeing to such requests without knowing the manner of that which was being asked of them. While frustrating, it was not unreasonable. I didn't even know what Dr. Levick had in store for them.

Until finally, a drunkard, who simply introduced himself as "Thompson" agreed to be our subject with the caveat that it would not include anything of a lewd or salacious act. Although unsure of the exact details myself, I was confident that nothing of the sort would be involved. Thompson was a slovenly and portly fellow with a thick, graying mustache and swollen features. He rarely spoke above a mumble and cast a sour odor from his tattered clothing. When we arrived at the lab, Dr. Levick was ecstatic. Like a fluttering hummingbird, Dr. Levick began to brief Thompson with his typical neurotic ramblings. Unable to keep maintain attention, the hobo nodded along as if he understood. The uncomprehending Thompson was, at last led over to the desk and was seated before the black mirror.

"I am going to inject you with a very miniscule dose of fish oil. Do not be alarmed, it is not lethal, however you will shortly feel the effects," Levick explained, his hand on Thompson's shoulder. Thompson nodded and Dr. Levick pulled a syringe from his back apron. The needle plunged into his arm as Levick slowly squeezed the plunger, injecting its contents into the man's blood stream.

"Fish oil?" I whispered

"A blend of my invention containing Tetrodotoxin. Extracted from a breed of fish the Japanese call Fugu. It is not yet known here in the western world," Levick whispered (repetition of whispered, perhaps use another word?) into my ear.

The rotund derelict began to convulse and foam at the mouth. With each twitch his body became more rigid, not even able to shift his gaze. The Doctor caught his falling head before it collided onto the desktop and gently set it down.

"The metal cart, please roll it over here." Levick pointed to the far side of the room.

The cart's wheels clacked on the tiles as I rolled it briskly across the floor and over to him. He pulled back the draped cloth to reveal a disturbing array of various tools. Augers, claws, toothed clamps and hooks. He grabbed a leather lash from the end of the tray and began to whip the paralyzed man in rapid succession. Still conscious but frozen in place, Thompson was as a sedated lab rat, with Levick's strikes snapping against the flesh of his back. After several minutes of the lashing, Levick looked up in excitement to notice slight movement from the metal orbs and tuning forks.

"Yes! Yes! Here, quick! Take the lash and continue probing the subject!" Dr. Levick shouted as he handed me the whip.

I continued to beat Thompson with the same timing in order not to disrupt the experiment. Dr. Levick ran over to the mirror as it started to blur and swirl.

"Yes! Hello? I am Dr. Levick, can you hear me? Can you see me?" he said frantically with his hands on the glass.

"Harder! Beat him harder!" Levick shouted.

My swings became swifter and more heavy-handed as the various contraptions began to resonate with increasing intensity. There was a similar vibration in the room to when the strange woman performed her meditations. The Doctor's excitement rose as apparitions began to form from the swirling abyss in the mirror. Then abruptly it all stopped, and the bowels of a now lifeless Thompson evacuated down his trouser legs and onto the floor. His limp body tilted sideways and collapsed onto the hard tiles. Vacant and bulging bloodshot eyes stared up towards the ceiling.

"No! No! You pathetic lout!" Thompson's hefty corpse wobbled with each of Dr. Levick's enraged kicks. He stopped to take a deep breath and regain his composure.

"Wasn't that magnificent?! A failure of an experiment but not fruitless. This has proved my theory correct! Concentrated suffering activates the mirror. It must be the vibrations in the aether? Or perhaps it's the heightened bio-electric response? We're going to find out. But my hunch was right! That's all that matters. We're going to need some time to concoct an even more effective method." Levick was rambling, standing over the tortured body.

"And what about Thompson?" I asked.

"Thompson? Oh, the subject. Yes, an unfortunate end. Please, dispose of it, if you don't mind," he said.

A cold chill went up my spine as I looked down upon the purpling face of Thompson which was now frozen into a twisted expression of hideous anguish. In the heat of the moment, I failed to realize the gravity of the situation. It was pure rapture, my adrenaline was at its peak and this poor delinquent was a mere subject, or shall I say *object*, to be used for our experimentation. A human being reduced to the status of a frog to be dissected in order to venture further into our Faustian thirst for discovery. It is unlikely anyone would miss or notice a street dweller like Thompson. But I couldn't help but question the ethics of this. Furthermore, what chilled me most of all was Dr. Levick's dispassionate reaction. A corpse lay before him, yet he had no panic, nor anxiety. We were now murderers, but no such consideration entered his mind. I worried that his obsession with this thesis was corrupting his ethics. Or worse perhaps, he never had any to begin with. He did, after all, shroud all of this in secrecy. Did he know the trajectory of this path would yield such monstrous fruits? It is unlikely a man of his intellect wouldn't be able to foresee such outcomes. Or perhaps, worst of all, that I too, was a mere subject in Dr. Levick's machinations.

If the latter was indeed true, I had no recourse. If I was to go to the authorities, it was I who lured the man to his doom, and it was I who held the lash in his final moments. Even a bum deserves greater dignity in his final moments than what we gave ol' Thompson. I can't think of a crueler death if I am being honest. Trapped within the prison of your own flesh, unable to move, unable to scream. Having full awareness and sensation while being methodically beaten like a dusty rug. It was barbaric in ways that would make a medieval dungeon guard squirm. Even if equal punishment was awarded to both Dr. Levick and I, the stain of shame upon my family for being involved in torturing and murdering a man would be ineluctable. And if indeed we ended standing before a judge, whom would they have believed? The brilliant and prestigious Dr. Piers William Levick? or me? A nameless student desperate for accolades in a highly competitive field. My fate was already set in motion. I was at the mercy of Dr. Levick's vision. A pawn in his enterprises and what hath been woven for us by the Moirai is now inexorably conjoined.

It was a burdensome and grim task to dispose of Thompson.

Even the most Herculean of grips would have found hoisting his carcass a troublesome feat. To ease the awkward sway of his lifeless limbs, I wrapped him in burlap and bound him head to toe in hemp rope. Using a rafter-fastened pulley, I lifted his shrouded body into an old wooden cart. I then chained him to a concrete block and covered the entire cart with a canvas tarp. Under the cover of night, I wheeled it to an old boat dock and tipped it. I miscalculated the buoyancy of the corpse and watched as the wrapped body of Thompson slowly floated downcurrent like a piece of wayward driftwood until he was out of sight. For the first time in broad memory, I said a prayer for Thompson's soul. And for mine.

As the weeks went on, Dr. Levick grew ever more neurotic and avoidant in divulging the details of his theory. My disposition on the matter of Thompson must've been obvious to him as his trust in me waned. But not in regard to my involvement in executing the experimentation. He was clearly concerned about protecting his research. I would oft look over to find him nervously hunching over his writings, protecting them from my possible gaze even when I was nowhere in the vicinity. Rarely would more than a few moments pass between his paranoid eyes shifted to the side to monitor my movements. Increasingly his concern for possible "plagiarists" became a frequent topic in our discussions. We both became truants and left the lab less and less as the days passed. I would oft wake in the night to find Dr. Levick pacing and rambling under his breath. I was unsure he slept at all as the color in his complexion became yellowish and pale and his figure became more emaciated. I too wasted in health and form as I spent my days fulfilling tasks of scouring books and retrieving equipment for his next experiment.

Even during the most mundane assignment, he would reiterate with nauseating repetition about the plagiarists. As if the omnipresent gaze of these caitiffs was waiting to strike the moment a cloth was lifted for too long or a page was left uncovered. The plagiarists were always watching, even when he was alone in a locked room. I very much enjoyed my time away from the lab where I could smell the fresh air and hear the voices of others as they spoke of even the most rudimentary things. As I was standing in line at the grocer, I overheard an elderly woman discuss her recipe for poppyseed muffins. It wasn't the allure of hot muffins that intrigued me but the sound and cadence of how she spoke. It was almost like a symphony beckoning me to reclaim my humanity. The isolation in the lab clouded my mind and plunged me into a numbing, depressive state. I suddenly had the urge to run. To flee back to my family estate and confess it all to my father. I am his son after all. Perhaps he would protect me if I admitted that I was manipulated and coerced by Levick. But, nevertheless, I played this fantasy in my head as I slavishly marched back to the lab with a satchel full of canned food. And like every time before, Levick hurried me inside before scanning up and down the alleyway for lurking plagiarists and locking the door shut with a series of deadbolts.

I installed more pulleys, wheeled in five, seven-foot-tall glass vats and stacked jugs with various odd fluids in them. I built a rack in order to stack four-foot-long rods of magnesium about half an inch in circumference. Under close instruction, I climbed a wood ladder and dumped exact amounts of different liquids into the large glass tubes. Formic acid, saline solution and gelatin, among other ingredients, were poured into the vats creating a foul-smelling slurry that I mixed with a long boat oar. After each use, the oars had to be sanitized in a pot of boiling water and alcohol. After several days of preparation, Dr.

Levick's next task was to acquire more subjects. Five subjects in total. It was at this moment I realized that these five vats of concoction were going to house five unknowing subjects.

"I can't do it. I can't lure more men to their deaths," I said.

"I'll tell you what you can't do, my boy. You can't renege now. I assure you; this is the finale. The final experiment to bring this all together. Don't you want to be here when we make the greatest discovery of human history?!" Levick explained with wild eyes.

"Thompson now floats in the Delaware river because of me. He was a living breathing man and now he is feeding the fish," I said with swelling eyes.

"Who? Thompson? That fat cretin? A worthy end to a meaningless life. He died for something far greater. When we show the world what we're about to uncover, there will be no regard for the lives of derelicts. He feeds the fish now. It was only a few winters until he fed the rats," he argued.

"Dr. Levick, I have surely been expelled from the university, I am going to be shunned by my family. I must draw the line here," I said.

"Draw the line? Okay, I will now draw you a line. I have here, a few bottles of whiskey. In them is a dose of chloral hydrate. You are going to take them and give them to five derelicts. A few minutes after they drink them, they will be unconscious. You will then load them up into your cart and bring them back here," Levick said.

"I refuse. And if you try to force me, it will come to blows," I threatened with clenched fists.

Dr. Levick drew a revolver from his waist "No. No it will not. You are going to complete this last assignment. And if you do not return in two hours' time, I will inform the police of your crime. You see, young man. Every document in this lab and the ones I've placed among your belongings back at the university, are signed with your name that I copied from our contract. Every piece of evidence demonstrates that this entire experiment is of your invention," he explained deviously, with his revolver pointed at my chest.

"What?! But why?! What about the plagiarists? I thought this was your life's work?" I asked in a panic.

"A means to an end. None of this will matter. Papers and studies and endless superfluous discourse speculating the most tedious details of mundanity. All filth! Science is just pigs rolling back and forth in their own mud. Now they speak of progress and revolution. As if that isn't more of the same. We, my boy. We are going to speak with God!" he shouted, with ecstasy in his deranged eyes.

There was no way out. My naivety had led me into the web of a predator. A psychopath of the highest order. I was first enamored by his unorthodoxy and prestige and then simply considered him a victim of his own genius. I pitied him, thinking he had sunk into an obsession and gone mad. But I was correct in my worst fears. He *was* mad from the moment I met him. He carefully selected me due to my desperation and desire to pursue an easy path to esteem. He knew that my status as a blue blood would cloud my judgment as I would be concerned with familial ramifications. And he predicted that I wouldn't detect the scheming motives behind his behaviors. I was unsure how much of this was an act and what was genuine. My discernment between truth and untruth began to unravel in my sleep deprived mind. The isolation, the sleepless nights, how much of it was by design to procure me? How much of it was authentic? I couldn't know, I couldn't tell. Was that part of his plan as well? To incrementally separate me from normalcy in all fashions? Even detach me from my ability to discern reality itself?

I wasn't sure if I seduced myself with false logic or if the prospects of the conclusion Dr. Levick described truly excited me. But I went to the streets in the dark of night with enthused vigor and did exactly as he commanded. With relative ease I found five drunkards, gave them their drink with the deception that I can't partake without the bedevilment of a tyrannical wife. With little argument they all drank and one by one, they all fell unconscious. I stacked them into my cart, covered them and wheeled them back to the lab. It was near comical that no policeman stopped me, and no passerby even looked suspiciously as I wheeled a cart of sedated bodies around the city streets. One instance a man even stopped to ask me if I needed a hand. In lackadaisical fashion, he leaned upon my cart and told me about his time as a laboring youth. I briefly indulged him and apologetically explained that I'm on a short schedule and must be home to study. The man tipped his hat and commended me for my work ethic.

Upon returning to the lab, Dr. Levick had already prepared what was needed to continue the experiment. We placed a rubber breathing hose down their throats and sealed their nostrils with glue and staples. We then wrapped them in porous burlap and bound them in hemp rope. An extra length of rubber band was used to pull their heads down in a permanent chin tucked position. With use of the pulleys, we lowered them one by one into the vats of fluid with breathing hoses draped over the sides. After a few hours each of the men awoke and began to panic as they realized they were bound, blind and submerged. Most of them gave up within an hour however, one of them flailed rather ferociously throughout the night. But, after realizing no escape was possible, surrendered to just float, suspended in the fluid. When walking by the vats, near the breathing tube, one could hear the deep labored breaths of the men. Dr. Levick made it a point to ensure that each man stayed alive. This close monitoring went on for several days until the heavy breathing reduced to gentle breaths and the occasional panicked kicks became involuntary twitches.

Every third morning, Dr. Levick would climb the ladder and stab a footlong needle down into the shoulder flesh of one of the subjects. On the first, the subject reacted with noticeable recoil. Several weeks passed of monitoring and probing the subjects. Day by day the relationship between me and Levick began to improve once again. We exchanged stories, had laughs and even spent a night or two partaking in a few pints of beer as we did back in the university hall. He apologized for the encounter with the revolver and claimed that if the situation would have escalated, he would have lost his greatest pupil and colleague. I knew in the back of my mind that he was a madman holding me with threat of coercion. But I couldn't help but feel elevated by his words. It was at that moment, that I realized, I too, was a madman. Yes, Dr. Levick extorted me. Yes, he manipulated me. But it was I who stayed. It was I who had forgone these supposed ethics and morals I pretended to be outraged about it in my own mind. This entire time I feared the repercussions of disappointing my family. I scurried in the shadow of my father knowing that they expected me to just meet the bare expectations in order to gain my inheritance. To shovel me off to school in hopes that I retrieve a pittance of accomplishment to not embarrass them. Well, it is they who disappoint me. They shall grovel at my feet when Dr. Levick and his vision comes to fruition. All of their meager earthly efforts will be but a squirt of piss in the face of a man who has spoken with God.

On the fifth week, Dr. Levick probed the first subject to find a fascinating discovery. As he plunged his needle into the shoulder flesh of the still breathing subject, there was no reaction. Breathing accelerated but no physical reaction was apparent. In addition, Levick could drive the needle into the flesh until he ran out of length.

"It is time, my boy! It is time! Hoist the subjects and suspend them by the mirror. We can unwrap them and let them dry." He shouted.

I did as I was told and hoisted the subjects out of the vats using the pulley. The stench was pungent and sharp like pickled, rotten meat. After cutting the ropes and carefully unwrapping the men from their soaked shrouds, their appearance was quite peculiar. Despite the faint breathing of the subjects, there was no motion from the chest cavity. They were deathly still. Their skin had taken a pale and dark greenish character and those with open eyes were unblinking. Despite being swollen and discolored, the men were alive and breathing. Frozen like pickled (you've used pickled twice here, perhaps substitute another word like 'vinegared'?) statues of inanimate flesh. The Doctor and I <u>dabbed</u> them dry with cloths as they slowly spun and swayed suspended by hooks with their heads facing downward.

"Grab the breathing hose and listen for a change in pace" Levick requested.

I placed my ear to the hose as he pulled a carving knife from his wheel cart. He slowly sliced a finger from the rigid hand. The breathing accelerated as his knife passed through the man's flesh, severing the finger. He was as still as a statue. Dr. Levick came over and placed the severed finger into my palm. Upon inspection, I noticed the texture of the flesh was strange. No bleeding as the blood was coagulated into a similar texture as the flesh. It resembled a piece of soft cheese.

"This is amazing. No bleeding? And they're still alive?" I asked.

"Yes. Their internal systems are still intact. They can breathe and feel sensation. However, the solution has softened their flesh and much of their skeletal structure," he explained.

"So, they can still feel pain, but they can't go into shock," I said.

"Precisely! Now for the finale, my boy. We're going to take those magnesium rods and plunge them behind their necks. Be very careful not to damage or make contact with the spine. You're going to press them down until just above the tailbone." he said.

"And then what?"

"And then one by one we're going to light the magnesium rods. They will slowly spark and burn, melting the flesh away inch by inch for hours. We angled their heads downward so that it wouldn't burn into their skulls and kill them. Each subject should give us approximately six hours of concentrated suffering," Levick continued.

"Human candles..." I uttered with an astonished smile.

"Right! Brilliant!" he exclaimed.

"Can they hear us?" I asked

"Let's hope not. Lord wouldn't that be cruel," he said as we both laughed.

With surgical care I took the magnesium rods and plunged them down into the flesh of the subjects. I could hear their breathing accelerate but couldn't help but feel detached from these human candles. As if their humanity was already removed. Or perhaps it was my humanity that was removed. Nevertheless, I carried out my task with perfect form. The rods were stabbed down into the spines of subjects. Their panicked breathing created a disjointed rhythm as they slowly rotated in the air. Dr. Levick dragged his chair to go sit before the mirror and ~~sat there staring~~ stared into its reflective black in silence for a few moments.

"Light the first one and then another after that one has burnt to completion. Let's try that in succession," he called to me.

I lit the first magnesium rod. It sparked and burned until

the hot glow made contact with the flesh. I could hear as labored breaths became more and more intense. At a snail's crawl, the glow melted away the skin around it, exposing pink jelly and vertebrae. The tuning forks, hanging spheres and other instruments began to vibrate and spin about with an intensity we had not yet seen. Abyssal swirls and patterns began to appear in the mirror to Levick's excitement. He started again with his lines of basic questions attempting to get a reply. After a few hours a disembodied figure formed from the mutating shapes and patterns in the mirror's glass.

"Yes! Hello! I am Dr. Piers William Levick, can you hear me?" he stated

A ghostly sepulchral tone vibrated from the mirror in stuttered syllables. A hideous choir of disharmonious pitches spoke forth in alien tongue. It responded but not in any recognizable human language. A series of low hum shrieks and guttural trills. The figure's visage of stewing gray cloud, splitting, forming and folding in on itself into an ominously expressionless face with simultaneously too many and too few features. Dr. Levick fell to his knees before the chthonic incorporeal entity with tears of joy streaming down his face.

"Yes! Please, my lord! Show me!" he begged

His crying joy became confused panic as his arms jerked towards the mirror with otherworldly force. His hands bent backward as the skin around his forearms accordioned, splintered shards of shattered bone stabbed through his flesh. A blood curdling roar of terror echoed from his mouth as his torso sucked against the glass with a terrible magnetic pull. His screams pitched upward and became muffled as his ribcage flattened with a wet crunch. The skin around his skull ripped away exposing the pink, white bone underneath. The soft flesh of his belly split and peeled back as the ropey contents of his insides were torn out and sucked into the mirror. I ran over as his body was twisting and breaking in ghastly ways and being pulled into the glass by the entity as it continued speaking in its ancient funereal tongue. I leaped to grab the last flap of wet flesh. I dug my fingers into the eye sockets of a formless face, but it was ripped from my clutches and drank (sank?) into the mirror. I heard the clang of the rod's iron core onto the tile floor as all commotion abruptly ceased as it did with prior experiments. The mirror was now blank again and the room was eerily still. I turned around and stared vacantly at the human candles suspended in air, slowly rotating, the rhythm of their labored breaths amplified in the empty room. I began to feel lightheaded and made a few steps towards the desk to sit down. I lost balance and fainted before I could sit, hitting my head on the thick plane of the desktop.

While unconscious I dreamed something that I cannot recall. It was a near schizophrenic fever dream of fragmented memories and anxieties to which the details probably couldn't be articulated even if I could recollect it. All of the days and weeks of sleeplessness and exhaustion overcame me, and I laid there for hours. Eventually I pulled myself up and lumbered over to my cot. In a slumbering comatose, my body forced me to recover all of my lost energy. With no discernment of time or day I finally arose. I cranked open a can of luncheon meat and a can of cold peas. I ate them slowly as I gazed upon the oddities of the human candles and the used subject with his spine cavity carved out exposing a burnt spinal cord. I paced back and forth conspiring and pontificating. There was no other way than to continue the experimentation myself. If the authorities were to enter this lab they would find a disheveled young man, a few hanging pickled corpses and a bloodstain in front of a mirror. Are they supposed to believe that the great Dr. Piers William Levick was sucked into another dimension by some extraplanar entity? And if they did believe it, I would surely be labeled as a practitioner of witchcraft surrounded as I was by this morbid display.

So, I gathered myself and decided I would continue on. I lit the first subject and walked over to the chair where Levick had been sitting before his demise. I sat with pen and paper to record the interactions with whatever strange entity I encountered, be they angel or devil or other. As before the instruments began to react with a now familiar intensity. The mirror came to life. I braced myself for my final moments, expecting an ethereal entity to pull me into its immaterial realm. I sat and stared into the swirling mists of the mirror until a figure formed that horrified me in a way that I couldn't fathom. It was Dr. Levick. The entity shimmered spectrally but it was recognizably him as I had known him. He was a discolored monochromatic gray, similar to the other manifestation.

"Hello, my boy! Dr. Levick at your thervith." He spoke jovially but in a haunting disembodied tone.

I spoke clearly with the apparition of Dr. Levick, and he responded as he would have in life. I began with a line of questioning to confirm his identity. Although I am not a religious man, I come from strong protestant roots. I know that demons are known for their deception. But he answered in ways that satisfied my suspicions. At least to a degree that could be known. I then continued to ask where he was and if he had met God. The answers were cryptic and unsatisfactory. To both he answered simply "it's complicated". But he then divulged that beyond this world there is one where the confinements of reality do not exist. Constraints such as time and locality are not present. I asked if he was in Heaven or Hades or a realm of the dead. To which he again responded that "it's complicated". I sat and noted everything he told me until six hours had gone by, and he vanished from the glass.

I took a short rest and pondered over the results until lighting another subject. The familiar effects on the instrumentation began once again. And as before, an apparition of Dr. Levick appeared from the cloudy phantasmal forms. However, this time he seemed less of himself. Instead of avoidant responses, he would stay silent. When he did respond, those responses took longer than before. The expressions upon his face grew fainter and less pronounced. After our second meeting I repeated the process and with each session he grew more estranged and less responsive. The sound of his voice became ever more aberrant and hollower. Often Levick would not even make eye contact, instead, he stared through me as if I wasn't there. Upon lighting the fifth and final subject, it took a great deal of time for him to appear. His visage was abnormal and elongated. There was no humanity behind his fading eyes as he stared blankly into the distance. He said nothing this time. And after ignoring my first few questions, he slowly dissipated. Sinking deep into the fogs of some unknown abyss.

Despite this, my mirror scrying sessions with the apparition of Dr. Piers William Levick, had bestowed upon me some disturbing knowledge. While I had retrieved little in the way of what strange otherworld he was pulled into or who or what resides there, he had told me what to expect from the passage of time.

As I write this, it is now September of the year 1898. In less than two decades the world will be consumed into a terrible war of nations. Countries will be redrawn, and all the standing noble houses of Europe will be dethroned. Many of whom will be brutally slaughtered. From the ashes of this catastrophe a group of great leaders will rise to restore the order of the old world. They will fail and their countries will be annihilated with fire from the sky. The survivors of those nations will be subjugated in unimaginable ways. Thus will come a century of evil reign at the hands of blood-drinkers. In their hubris the vampires will create thinking machines that then enslave them. Mankind will relinquish their humanity and become twisted subhumans. There will be no more nations nor kings nor rule of law. The sun will go into a deep slumber and all the world will become a frozen tomb of endless winter. Mankind will perish forever in less than two centuries from now.

I have been wandering the streets of Philadelphia and in my distress of this knowledge I have made the mistake of divulging it to a gathering of pub goers. They found my grave warnings of the future to be quite amusing and farcical as I expected. However, after confessing to how I know such things, they found it mortifying. I am certain that they have alerted the authorities who will inevitably find our lab and the remnants of the human candles. What will befall me upon arrest will be a fate worse than death. The public will not understand what we have done here in our quest for scientific discovery and my family will surely disown me. I have found Dr. Levick's revolver among his belongings and with it will exit this world upon my own volition.

I pray that these writings will not be lost to history or be destroyed. I pray that I am looked upon not as a madman, but a true scientific mind misled by my own ambitions. In the desk drawer you will find an envelope containing the last savings of both myself and Dr. Levick that I withdrew posthumously. I bequeath this and any and all assets in my name to the families of the men who are deceased as a result of our experiments, including the one named Thompson.

The transcription of my sessions with the apparition of Dr. Levick and all other accrued research may be found in the case beneath the desk. This is my last accord. Please pray that I find mercy in the next world.

I am sorry I have failed you father,
Henry Jacob Wharton IV

Thank you for reading

I'm just a guy who loves this. I love tales of heroes and monsters and ancient magic. I love poetry and the sounds of words. I love beauty and weirdness. I am an autodidact with no formal education from very meager upbringing. I know that what I do is very antiquated in both style and format. Very few people read written works anymore. And even fewer read the kind of stuff that I write.

So thank you for buying my little book and giving me your time to hopefully entertain you in some fashion. I pray that you enjoyed.

Blessings to all of you,
    Dave Martel

Printed in Great Britain
by Amazon